THE BENEFICIARIES

Sarah Penny was born in Cape Town, South Africa, in 1970. She studied at the University of Cape Town, Rhodes University and St Andrews University, Scotland, migrating to the UK in 2003 to lecture in Creative Writing at Brunel University London, where she completed her PhD on sangomas (traditional African healers).

Sarah has three children and lives in North London, but still travels regularly to South Africa. When not writing and teaching, she works with communities, mainly in African countries, using arts for social change.

The Beneficiaries

SARAH PENNY

Valley Press

First published in 2002 by the Penguin Group
Penguin Books (South Africa) (Pty) Limited

This revised edition first published in 2019 by Valley Press
Woodend, The Crescent, Scarborough, YO11 2PW
www.valleypressuk.com

ISBN 978-1-908853-93-6
Cat. no. VP0110

Cover design by Jamie McGarry. Text design by Jo Haywood.
Cover photographs by Fernando Weberich and Pierre Amerlynck.

Printed and bound in Great Britain by
Imprint Digital, Upton Pyne, Exeter.

Supported using public funding by
ARTS COUNCIL
ENGLAND
LOTTERY FUNDED

for the Kingwills
of The Rest, Nieu Bethesda,
for many years of friendship

'The truth is validated by the majority, they say. Or you bring your own version of the truth to the merciless arena of the past – only in this way does the past become thinkable, the world become habitable.'

Antjie Krog, *Country of my Skull*

Part One

A Letter

This least sought-after of requests concludes:

The thing which I ask I wish for the memory of my child and for my own rest.

uTixo abenawe,
Nomda Qhashane

'I won't do it,' says the recipient quite loudly, although there is no one to hear and, beyond that, no one to say that one ought. Having snatched the post in passing from the mail tray in the house lobby she is out on the street already, and some careless person has burned through the only street bin with hot ash. Fortunately, further along the street there is a big private bin in somebody's front yard. She backhands the letter surreptitiously into its open mouth, although the black bags have already been gathered for the day by the borough service, so that it remains there until the next collection – a forlorn cream envelope slightly sullied with potato peelings.

1998

Contact

Why did she phone? Truth is, she doesn't know. A scrap of paper, casually given, lay for some months in a leather handbag.

'Pim,' she says.

She hears hesitation. Then:

'Lally?' Budding into astonishment.

'Laeticia,' she says. 'Hello, Pim.'

'I go by Edgar,' he says.

A bus across London. Magnolia trees flaunting their indelicate petals at the asphalt. The sky is a neutral canvas of the chillier shades of blue, across which aeroplanes leave vapour wakes of purpose.

The house is in one of the twisting urban lanes off the Fulham Road. She recognises the area as being fashionable for people who don't use the word 'fashionable'. She counts off the numbers as she makes her way along the road. Pim's has a half-moon of stained glass over the front door – opaque, azure and burgundy. Cacti in the front yard are reluctantly adapting to their waterlogged conditions.

She has her finger on the button. Footsteps echo down a flight of stairs and along a passageway. The door opens awkwardly over a resistant tongue of carpet.

Edgar-who-was-Pim is fatter than one might have remembered, but also sleeker. He ushers Laeticia-who-was-Lally inside.

'I was sorry to hear,' he says formally.

She would be masterful, but is betrayed by her eye-brows.

'About your father,' Pim explains.

Ah. Of course, there are social forms.

'Congratulations,' she offers. Her slight hands, gesturing at the slick of photographs on the walls, cover all felicities.

They look at each other.

'It *has* been a long time,' he says, like an Englishman.

Spuds and lineage

'Ruth can transform a potato,' Ruth's mother likes to say.

Ruth, who is fond of her mother, thinks it a silly remark nevertheless. But now: 'Ruth can transform a potato,' says Pim.

In marriage, words are currency – each one carrying a weight beyond the sum of its parts. In the Ruth/Pim union there are some utterances that belong to Ruth and some to Pim. Ruth doesn't know why Pim said 'Ruth can transform a potato' – a sentence borrowed from his mother-in-law – but she doesn't like it.

'I can't cook a thing,' says Lally. 'Actually, I don't like eating much. Once I didn't eat at all for weeks and weeks, and eventually I fell over and they put me on a drip.'

'I remember that,' says Pim. 'You were very silly.'

'Yes,' agrees Lally. 'Yes – I expect I was.'

'What was in the drip?' asks Ruth's elder son.

'Sugar,' says Lally vaguely. 'Something like that.'

'I had an injection,' announces the elder son importantly. 'Didn't I, Daddy? In my arm, when we went to Africa.'

Ruth gets up and clears the serving dishes away, stacking

them next to the sink. They're eating in the kitchen because Edgar wanted to eat with the children. Ruth isn't crazy about the direction the conversation is taking. She feels marginalised in her own home.

The extraordinary potatoes – white clouds streaked with cheesy infusions – steam gently on the quintet of plates. Pim has taken the spoon away from his younger son and is levering the pulp into the child's mouth. The boy protests, struggling for possession of his spoon. He knows exactly what to do with it. But Pim is being vigorous about his role as husband and father tonight.

'Our grandpa's got a farm in Africa,' offers the elder son.

'Yes, I know – I used to visit there when I was your age.'

'You don't know how old I am!'

She doesn't dispute this, but she doesn't give him the spur he's waiting for either.

'I'm seven,' announces the elder son indignantly. 'Did you visit when you were seven?'

Was she seven? Yes – five to seventeen; all the years she lived institutionally. All the exeats, the short holidays. Her own farm; poorer, dustier, too far distant to make the journey.

'Do you have a farm?' prompts the boy. He is at an age where he likes to hero-worship, and Lally is under consideration for the evening.

Are children always this indefatigable? 'Yes,' says Lally.

'Is it goats, like Grandpa's?'

'No,' says Lally. 'Ostriches.'

The boy's cherry mouth forms a circle. He can see them now – fiercely-feathered oblongs hurtling at briar fences on garden-rake legs. Lally has hit a home-run as an unwilling contender in the hero stakes.

She has not, in fact, visited her farm in over five years. Her farm is an envelope of figures which she receives each month from the manager because her widowed mother (since re-established in town) is now too elderly and blighted to take an interest. Lally isn't interested either, but the manager is a man of duty.

'How is Pim?' says Lally to Pim, by way of changing the subject. Every first-born male in Pim's family has been called Pim since the first Pim acquired the nickname on the ship on the way out. Reasons lost in the fog of coasts hugged or times gone past. There are seven Pims – one in London (alive), one on the farm (alive), four on the farm (dead), one in a forgotten field of France (dead). Lally means the live, farm-bound Pim – father of Pim the Londoner.

'He's fine.' Pim gives up on his force-feeding scheme. 'There was a lot of stock theft. Michael's helping him.'

Pim's face is expressionless. Michael is Pim's younger brother. Pim is not unconscious of the heavy weight of history – the contravention of first principles that occurs when a Pim-destined farm is managed by a Michael.

'I'm a Pim,' says the elder son, unexpectedly. 'No, you aren't,' interrupts Ruth. 'And it's bedtime.'

'I *am* a Pim,' repeats the boy. He will not be prevented from claiming the romanticism of his birthright.

Ruth shepherds the children upstairs to clean their teeth. The aspirant Pim ravages at a bloodied pit that has lately appeared, while Ruth prods apart the milkier gums of the younger boy. Downstairs she can hear Edgar chatting to his peculiar friend.

'Mum!' grizzles the child, batting at the toothbrush with protesting hands. She realises she has hurt him. She crouches to put her arms around him, seeing in the mirror how the round arc of her chin fits into the pale curve of his shoulder, how her soft hair spills against the fresh skin of his back. *I'm still a young woman.* She's not quite thirty –

five years younger than Lally; ten years younger than Pim. In the further reaches of the mirror, her first son has imagined himself into an ostrich, his dressing gown deputising for feathers, toothbrush beak pecking grubs from the grout in the bathroom tiling.

1978

Standard Eight
Hadedas and Earthworms

Lally leans on the points of her elbows on the window sill, watching the hadedas feed on the hockey field below. They like to settle on the pitch after practice, when the drumming heels of the children have brought out scores of blindly deluded earthworms, puckering mucous mouths at the thought of rain. The hadedas are a dull pea-green, but at this distance they look black – or as if they are pretending to be not entirely black, like so many raffish undertakers. Two of the larger birds are scrapping, lifting in bursts of flight on flapping wings, their coarse belligerent shrieking scraping at the more dulcet harmonies of a country afternoon. Ugly birds. At home she picks them out of the sky with her pellet gun, watching their suddenly arrested flight; their last journey down to the veld and the grinning, sportive jaws of dogs.

The hockey field is flanked by the rugby field, the cricket pitch, the swimming pool and tennis courts. Seen from above, the squares in different colours resemble a disordered stretch of parquet flooring. Lally is on the third floor of the squat cement, brick and stone structure of the girls' division. Opposite – across the fields – is the mirrored functionalism of the boys' division. Between, giving on to the fields, is the red brick massif of the school block. Fifty years ago, there was only the school block, but the school has grown in popularity and the school block has been restricted to pedagogical purposes only. Lally's school, though not a private establishment, so nearly approximates one that its inmates don't mind revealing where they were schooled in their afterlives as alumni. It has history, in the colonial sense, and several endowments for the more deserving of its men to proceed to international education.

Lally shifts on the sill and draws a breath, the flares of her burgundy hockey skirt fluttering in a drift of wind. On certain sunny afternoons, like this one, heated pockets of air move lazily across the valley, conveying the ripe aromas of the farms that terrace the low hills and lead into the plains – the confident fragrance of oranges on trees, the hot waft of lucerne. It is that part of the recreational hour between practice and prep devoted to the distribution of tea. While the other children are out on the veranda with mugs of Ceylon and jam sandwiches, she prefers to be here in the unlikely silence of the briefly deserted room. In any case, she is one of those troublemakers down in matron's register as a difficult eater – to be weighed on Saturdays, and regularly apprised of the situation of children in Africa who have nothing to eat in the first place. At night, she likes to press a penlight torch to her own limbs under the covers – seeing the red glare of her illuminated flesh, the darker shaft of bone.

The east-facing room where Lally is escaping from tea is the Standard Eight dormitory. Each child has brought from home a bedspread in a personal colour, a selection of shorts and jeans and tee-shirts to wear as mufti between chapel and dinner on Sunday, and family photographs to pin to the noticeboards above the bunks. Lally has in her hand a letter from her parents – or, more precisely, her mother – who writes for both. Her mother's letters arrive reliably each week and always fall into three paragraphs:

news of the farm, news of the district and a response to whatever communications have been recently forwarded by Lally with attendant injunctions. *I was pleased to hear of your progress in history and mathematics, and will send a postal order for stockings, as yours are all worn through.* Lally reads the letter through twice and puts it back inside its envelope, and then inside a shoe box on a ledge at the top of her locker. She will take it out again at prep in order to write in return with reference to the key events of the letter. Lally will put her letter in the collection box at the back of the prep hall (which is also the dining hall), where it will wait with the other children's mail until the hostel mistress collects the box in the morning and delivers it to the post office. In the shoe box, there is a small hoard of envelopes which Lally's mother stamps and addresses to herself in order to facilitate the regularity of Lally's correspondence.

The ascendant stamping of the other children's feet can now be heard on the wooden stairs, and in twos and threes they arrive in the doorway, sticky with sweat and jam, and throw themselves chattering on to the beds. She smiles and moves away from the window. Because she is apart from the other children, her apprehension of them is imagistic – a blonde ponytail, a sunbrowned shank, a pair of spectacles, a grin of wired teeth. A jumble of parts, she sees them not as this one or that one, but as a moving current of intention in whose slipstream she will follow. She isn't, in fact, unpopular, or not noticeably unpopular, which is where the danger lies. And she knows how to behave. She keeps her bunk and locker immaculate and stays out of the way of the prefects. So that if you asked the other children, the worst they might say of her was that she was dull. And the boys leave her alone, not pretty enough to solicit, but not ugly enough to taunt. Anyway, she's been there as long as anyone, and longer than some.

She is, it appears, one of those children of whom one says years later: 'Oh, you'll never guess who I saw at such-and-such a place ... don't you remember – she had a bunk next to yours. Heavens, now – what was her name?'

On preferment

Emily is a matric, a girl two years older than Lally who is a whizz at tennis. Now she is standing in her whites at the top of the short flight of stairs that leads to the prefects' rooms in the attic, beckoning to Lally.

'Lal,' says Emily breathlessly, 'you must see!'

Lally mounts the steps with reserve. In institutional life, in any kind of life where a hierarchical order prevails, there is a geography of safety. The grey-carpeted corridor which Lally is leaving behind is an area for which she has full licence – more than licence – almost a prerogative to occupy. As long as it is not those pockets of time apportioned to prep or practice or school or meals, Lally could pass up and down this corridor a thousand times and no one can object. The corridor presents no choices, no risks, no evaluation. In traversing its length, she is doing nothing more or less than is required of her.

Yet the moment Emily makes the command, 'You must see!', Lally has to make a decision. She may ascend the staircase without jeopardy, since she is under the sufferance of Emily, a rightful occupier of the prefectural annexe above. But the instant her foot leaves the hairy gunmetal threads of the corridor carpet and finds itself on the gaudier florals of the stair upholstery, she makes an irrevocable adjustment to her position, trading in the certainty of right (all children of that age may be in that place at that time) for the vagaries of goodwill. More ominously, she moves from a position of anonymity (an obedient child in a corridor) to one of prominence (a junior in senior quarters by invitation).

There are of course in Lally's year those who would leap – who would take the steps two at a time, arriving on the landing in good cheer and wholehearted confidence. They are the children who want a bite of the cherry, who are reasonably convinced that with perseverance and manoeuvring they too might clamber up the skeins of the rope ladder of institutional success to enjoy, in their final year, those benefits parcelled out to the chosen. If Lally's foot wavers on the first step it is because she is not a cherry-biter, or is perhaps aware that she does not possess the qualities to be a cherry-biter. If there is one figure of fun in institutional life, it is a cherry-biter without qualities.

Yet if Lally were to refuse Emily's command/invitation she would equally draw attention to herself; an attention which without doubt would be actually, rather than potentially, hostile. So, there is really no option but to progress slowly forward to where Emily is standing in her skirt and singlet, slapping carelessly at a streamlined calf with the covered head of her racket.

'Come along,' urges the impatient senior, catching Lally by the sleeve of her tunic and pulling her into one of the dormer bedrooms. Sitting on a bed set against the window is Emily's room-mate (a girl from the Copper Belt in Zambia) and her next-door neighbour (the daughter of a diamond mining engineer). They both make a gesture of acknowledgement toward the new arrival, while Lally unhappily watches Emily's whitened tennis shoes carry her over the rug towards the bureau, where she locates a single photograph.

'Look,' cries Emily ecstatically to Lally, the girl from the

Copper Belt and the mining engineer's daughter. 'He's become an officer!'

Emily's patronage of Lally constitutes, in terms of the school, an unnatural act. Each yearly intake in a hierarchical system forms a self-enclosed and impermeable generation which makes Emily, effectively, Lally's grandmother. Why, then, did Emily choose to prise Lally from her natural habitat of the corridor to form this unprecedented and potentially hazardous anschluss in the prefects' quarters? It does, after all, undermine not only Emily's position (which she has voluntarily put under threat), but the sovereign authority of Emily's comrades, the girl from the Copper Belt and the mining engineer's daughter, who have at no point entered into an encouragement of Emily's impetuous solicitation. In fact, although Lally has only been in the room some several seconds, a dilemma has already presented itself to the mining engineer's daughter in the form of Lally's hemline which, if not actually loose, is delectably lopsided. The mining engineer's daughter (who can be as severe and proud as a stone) would have dispatched Lally to the needlework room with immediate effect, had she encountered the fault in any other territory but the supra corpus juris minefield of the prefects' quarters. Were she to issue such an instruction now, her order and Emily's command (even such an odd command as it was) would be at loggerheads, presenting a disunited front to the junior. So, she sits crossly against the pillow, not saying anything.

The photograph Emily holds in her hand is the clue, more than the clue, the raison d'être of the whole impasse. Emily's boyfriend is Pim, the eldest son of the family who acts in loco parentis to Lally over exeats and short holidays. This relationship has lasted for two years: the better part of Pim's prefecture in the boys' division and the first year of his conscription into the infantry. So that Lally and Emily have been thrown together on several occasions in the steadily recurring rhythms of Pim's farm – the rituals of breakfasts and dinners, of hunts and game drives. Emily never pays much attention to Lally when Pim is around, although any idiot could recognise that Lally's habitual startled rabbit performance on one side of the dining table nicely offsets Emily's girlish suavities on the other. Nevertheless, Pim is away fighting the enemy and Emily, in his absence, chooses to view Lally as a kind of de facto younger sister.

Lally, the girl from the Copper Belt and the mining engineer's daughter bend their heads over Pim's photograph. He is relaxed but alert, smiling at the photographer. A soldier's smile; arrogantly philanthropic, off to give the glory of his youth for the national good, his single lieutenant's star firmly clinched to his shoulder.

'Oh, Emily,' breathes the girl from the Copper Belt, who doesn't have a sweetheart. Lally makes a muted, appreciative noise. She doesn't like Pim, who is one of those guffawing, hearty boys always appearing in school plays hammed up as a nurse or carrying the banner while the brass band plays *When The Saints Go Marching In*. She prefers his brother Michael in the class above her, a quieter and more studious boy who likes to walk about the farm with a glass jar, measuring the health of the soil by capturing the resident bugs.

The other prefects are all back from practice now, and they come crowding through the door, tennis whizzes and athletic whizzes, stooping over each other like puppies to see the photograph, their plaits and ponytails falling into each other's faces.

'Isn't he handsome! Where will he be sent? Will he get leave?'

Those who only have photographs of private soldiers or schoolboys glued to the inside front cover of their homework diaries clutch their schoolbags closer.

The new influx expands the number of witnesses to Lally's presence in the room, and the mining engineer's daughter cannot in good conscience neglect the issue of the hemline any further.

'Lally,' she says pointedly, and gives her an order mark for slovenliness, writing and tearing out a permission leaflet from her order booklet for Lally to visit the needlework room. Emily's attention is now entirely focused on the photograph's reception and the conflicting emotions (dudgeon at Pim's absence; pride at Pim's achievements) that are stirring in her soul. Lally hovers, wondering if she should excuse herself, but the mining engineer's daughter raises her eyebrows expectantly, so Lally makes her way back down the stairway without further hesitation.

Matrimony

'Laeticia,' says Greenbow, 'could I have the notice for Barkston Gardens?'

'It's on your desk, Mr Greenbow.' Lally watches his reflected lurking on the screen of her terminal.

'Eh?' He moves towards the front of the office, to where his commodious desk commands a view of Cromwell Road and its bedevilled rivers of honking morning traffic. 'Oh, so it is.' His eyes track down the sheet. *Kitchen: 12 ft by 5 ft, laminated rolltop work surfaces, power points (x3), twin sinks with separate taps and faultless drainage under, view to garden.*

'Oh, Laeticia.' His finger hovers and settles. 'You ought to have left a line here. Breaks it up a bit, eh? Bit cluttered as it is.'

'Yes, Mr Greenbow.' He always finds a mistake, only really giving it up once it's imperative that the notice goes into the catalogue. Not that she minds. She's paid by the hour, and she doesn't care how many times she does it over.

Why, wonders Greenbow, does she call him Mr Greenbow when he has so specifically paved the way for 'Tim?' Is she being chippy? No, it's different with these girls from Africa. They grow up with the old traditions – plenty of strap, although on the other hand they will do the most extraordinary things that an English person wouldn't. He's seen her kick off her shoes and curl her legs up underneath her like a Buddhist, scratching with abstract gorilla enthusiasm at the inside of her thighs on sticky afternoons with the fan not working. But something draws one. His little bush Victorian. He watches her too-thin back (bracketed by ribs) and the spill of her dark bobbed hair as she bends conscientiously over the keyboard.

Lally is drawing up a flyer that will be dispatched to every owner in a particular block of flats, in the hope of attracting a seller for a secure client. She's at the point now of only needing to change the address slightly before feeding the computer the print command and her hand moves routinely, almost without thought, between the keyboard and the mouse. She's been in this job and in London for six months, and is not discontented with either arrangement. It's her sixth time round in London, her sixth attempt at living there, not counting stopovers somewhere else en route. She's been here at seventeen, twenty-two, twenty-seven, thirty, thirty-two, thirty-five. She knows how the city works – she can find herself a job and a bedsit within a week, sign up for a course at the City Lit, look up old workmates and classmates and dig in for a while, believing wilfully in the concept of home. Until she gets bored with the strain of neurotic restlessness to which she is peculiarly prone. Waking up on November mornings to the scratchy drift of leaves blowing across pavements, and her skin crawling with accidie. But she's all right for now; she's all right for now.

Mr Greenbow is back in her terminal screen, jolly and jowly, with hand-written instructions on the back of an envelope. He inclines over her to give her her orders, bathing her workstation in a piquant mist of cologne.

'I've noticed that you never eat lunch,' observes Greenbow severely, straightening up. 'It takes a toll on the health, y'know. Thins the blood.'

His own stomach, comfortably rotund, could not offer better proof of sanguinity.

'You should let me take you out for a bite. There's a fabulous little *charcuterie* round the corner.'

'Do you eat out much?' asks Lally, which doesn't sound much like a put-down, but is instantly understood by both parties to constitute one.

'No,' says Greenbow, deflated. 'My wife is quite a keen cook.'

He always refers to his wife as *my wife,* without a name, as men do when they are trying to distance themselves from their spouses – the titular conquering the personal. He has, in fact, been faithful to his wife through fifteen years of marriage and a year of courtship, except for once, shortly after the birth of his second child, when he slept with a prostitute whom he thought was Portuguese but who, as it turned out, came from Walthamstow. That makes it sound more intentional than it was – what really happened was that *my wife* went to her mother in Sheffield for a fortnight and, unexpectedly, an old pal of Greenbow's from Stowe came to visit and Greenbow and the old pal got drunk and went out to a club where Greenbow had never been before, and where a Portuguese beauty was sitting on his lap as he was swigging champagne straight out of the bottle and saying '*Muito obrigada, Senhorita.*' And then he took her home and she was tossing her bountiful head of ebony hair over her shoulders and putting a rubber on him (he'd never used a rubber before), which wasn't very nice, although he managed (twice), even though he was as drunk as a lord and the last rubber broke, at which point she stopped being Portuguese and started quizzing him histrionically about his sexual history in the voice of a cleaning lady. In the morning, he woke up and she was putting on her stockings and going back to Walthamstow and demanding money, leaving him with the sheets and the wet patch, in which two question-mark-shaped hairs faced each other in a parenthesis of enquiry across a pinkish splash of something unidentifiable.

'Surely not,' thought Greenbow with a shudder, being a man who would rather forgo when Mrs Greenbow was incommoded. So, he pulled the sheets off the bed, and did the laundry for the first time in his married life.

'I don't cook,' says Lally.

Greenbow finds that arousing. After the blamelessness of blancmange, the sanctimony of soup and the heavy virtues of sponge puddings at Sunday dinners, he feels ready for a liberated, non-cooking woman.

'Perhaps,' suggests Greenbow, his eyebrows archly lifting to a central point, riven through by his frown-furrow, like a river-borne view of Tower Bridge admitting a steamer, 'you've not had anyone particular to cook *for?*'

'No,' agrees Lally, simply.

Matins

First rising for the girls' division is at 6.15am, but in the summer months Lally invariably gets up before that, stimulated by the dawn – the fierce linear pyre of orange that breaks suddenly and shockingly above the low hills to the east of the valley.

One privilege she has won for herself in a decade of boarding school is to have her bunk next to the window, and now she slips from beneath her blanket and kneels in her nightgown at the sill. The morning air is crisp and pungent with the scents of grass and flowering heath, and the sky is adopting a sheen of powdery cloudless blue where the more sombre bruises of night-blue are rapidly disappearing.

The white district still slumbers, but the township, sprawled across the river marshland to the south of the valley, is alive with the excited barking of dogs ending their lonely night vigils, and disintegrating drifts of woodsmoke from a thousand pots of *phutu* stewing over a thousand fires.

Closer at hand, lights are blazing in the windows of the boys' division. She can hear the thin wail of the wake-up siren, followed almost instantly by the clattering echo of feet on stairs. She imagines them queuing for the showers, the wincing contortion of their faces as the first icy smack of water hits their still drowsy skin, hands hurriedly soaping at limbs and bottoms so that they can retreat from the jet, stamping and grinning. Now they are piling out on to the rugby field in their khakis, as they do every morning, sorting themselves into their platoons, standing fixedly to attention as the cadet master, Major Carlton, comes striding magisterially over the lawns.

'Atten-*shun!*' bawls the major, and the boys are as straight as corn plants, eyes forward, arms plumb-lined to their sides. The major is moving expertly along the lines, checking out the condition of the troops. He finds a boy with a button missing and writes an order slip for jacks after breakfast, which he folds and puts into the boy's shirt pocket.

Lally grins maliciously from her vantage point – she doesn't like the boy, and will enjoy his discomfiture through the morning, like the others will mock as he leans forward with his ribcage pressed against the desk to keep the weight off the jack stripes, the shame of tears whelming irrepressibly in the corners of his eyes. The boys are marching now; a several-hundredfold machine of pressed khaki, with the major shouting stentorian orders from the front. He prides himself on not having to use a loudhailer, but his voice over the course of the hour grows increasingly cracked and squeaky and some braver boys, during the duller parts of lessons, have been known to take off the major's strained ten-to-seven bray.

The major is from Rhodesia, where the war is still raging and will rage for another two years, but last year he got a phone call while in the field announcing that his wife (whom he had left on the farm in the care of neighbours) had been dismembered, as had the neighbours. So, he collected his two young daughters from school in Salisbury and came down south. The major does not see this act as desertion – Rhodesia *will* fall, and if you ask him he will tell you why in unambiguous and emphatic adjectives.

Outnumbered! Under-prepared! Betrayed!

If you ask him 'betrayed by whom?' he will tell you, 'Her Majesty', and the perfidy of that royal personage is, of course, the crux of the whole matter.

But South Africa, as he tells his boys, has a better fighting chance. Anyway, our backs are against the wall; we're the last hope for the white man in Africa, and if this nation falls it won't be because the boys from this school were under-prepared!

Lally can see Michael marching. He's a lacklustre marcher – not lazy or clumsy, but he doesn't have Pim's precision and panache. He will never, like Pim, carry the Sword of Honour at the inter-schools parade. There arc four children in Pim's family – all boys. The next in line, Ross, is thirteen, and Lally's eyes strafe down the lines until she finds him – a maladroit, uncoordinated boy struggling to keep in step with the others. Six years from now, Ross will fail to get down when he should have got down, and will die painfully under a fever tree from septicaemia resulting from a shrapnel wound in the stomach lining, too full of pus by the time the orderlies arrive to be high priority. Oddly, there's something dead about him already, although he is incontestably alive; his dull blonde hair cropped close to his head and his flaked skin prematurely wizened by the sun.

The youngest son, by a long stretch, is Mark, who is only in the first year and is too small to be in the cadets. Often, Mark is observable in the window of the Grade One dormitory, his fleshy child's fingers webbed against the panes, enthralled by the cadets. Sometimes he even breaks out, running over the fields in his bare feet and flapping dressing-gown to kneel in the dew and watch. He should get jacks for that, but the mMajor has a soft spot for Mark and only slaps him on his rump.

'Your time will come, m'boy,' he says. 'Run along before matron catches you, or you'll be in hot water!'

Inside Lally's dormitory, a girl who is dreaming restlessly – fractured, almost-awake dreams – cries out in her sleep.

'Shut up!' says another girl irritably. She is wound up in

a cocoon of sheets, trying to savour every possible minute before the siren goes.

Outside, the marching has stopped and the boys are doing exercises. The major is sending his pimpled private soldiers in search of invisible Matabele lurking behind the goal posts. After a while, they divide into groups: some boys are the South African Defence Force, and others are the enemy. The SADF skirmishes forward through the dew in a low-slung leopard crawl, although not low enough in some cases.

'Bottom, Stonier, you blistering idiot!' bawls the major, and Stonier digs his testicles obediently into the grass cover. The SADF are slugging the enemy with their imaginary firearms now, and those impersonating the enemy are dying, as Africans are understood to, at a stroke, like impalas trapped by lions, without fussing about last words, because Africans think collectively and not individually, which makes them, the major stresses again and again, a formidable enemy in battle.

A series of mini-vans crawling up the slight rise toward the school heralds the arrival of the real Africans, who are singing but fall silent once they pass the gatepost. The vans pull up in front of the school block, and the passengers clamber out. Before dispersing, they attend to their clothing; to their wellingtons and their overalls and the *doeks* they tie over their heads to keep the dust from their hair. Beneath the white hierarchy of the school – the headmaster, teachers and hostel staff, school prefects, house prefects and ordinary pupils – there is another, black, hierarchy: a busy subterranean hive of groundsmen, gardeners and handymen, cooks, kitchen staff and cleaning staff. The children call the men who work in the grounds 'the garden boys', and the women who cook and serve 'the kitchen girls', but the women who clean in the school block and the hostels, with whom they have more direct contact, they call *sisi*, a Xhosa term for an elder sister.

The garden boys and the kitchen girls and the *sisis* disappear to their respective work zones as the wail of the wakeup siren for the girls' division cuts plangently through the air. The major calls the parade to attention to prevent the unnecessary diverting of focus which inevitably occurs when the private soldiers imagine they might catch a glimpse of the young women in their nightgowns through the inadequately reflecting windows. The year prefect arrives and switches on the light behind Lally, and girls are leaping from their bunks and racing to gain the showers, knowing that the first few litres of water will have benefited from an effective overnight residency in the heating cylinder. The daylight is whitening, and a vapoury pall signals the evaporation of the dew from the grass and the heathery embankments whose scent, thwarted by rising heat, becomes less piquant.

It's another day in Africa.

Spuds and freedom

At the back of the girls' dining room there is a wall chart with a map of the world on it. Next to the world map is a noticeboard, and underneath the noticeboard is a small table with pins and strips of red paper. The strips of paper have a Bible passage on them.

Have I not commanded you? Be strong and courageous. Do not be terrified, do not be discouraged, for the LORD your God will be with you wherever you go.
Joshua, Chapter 1, verse 9

34

If a friend or relative goes overseas on holiday, the children are allowed to write the traveller's name and destination on the back of the tract and pin it to the noticeboard until they return safely. Some of the teachers object to the habit because there is something Catholic about it, but it is a tradition, and traditions are what separate a fine school from a mediocre one. There are tracts devoted to England and France and America and even Australia, although Australia is different because people don't go there on holiday; they go there forever.

The world map is a large one, and the countries are in different colours so that even if you stand at the far end of the dining room you can work out where Brazil changes into Argentina and the United States into Canada. Because the world map is situated directly in the middle of the back wall, the sun shining through the opposite window creates a sheen on its laminated paper surface at certain times of the day, and the position of the sheen also changes according to where one is sitting in the dining hall.

Once a fortnight the children are reassigned to tables. For most of them, their primary concern is who their new dining companions are – if they have butterfly elbows, are gobblers or bag all the syrup before one's even had a chance to reach for the jug. Because Lally's down in matron's register as a difficult eater, she always has to sit next to the prefect at the head of the table, who usually executes her duties by stabbing her fork suggestively at Lally's plate at sporadic intervals. The wolf-keen eyes of the other children rove between Lally's plate and the prefect, and when the prefect is momentarily distracted, Lally's scrambled eggs will miraculously reduce by two-thirds and her sausage, sliced with lightning speed into three parts, will be under assault by three steadily moving sets of jaws. If it's fish and chips or shepherd's pie (the prime favourites), the smallest children might be bribed to ask the prefect to pour their milk for them or tie their shoelaces.

Lally is more or less oblivious to her boosted popularity in the dining hall. She is overwhelmingly diverted by the wall map and its subtly altering permutations. She knows, for example, that if she is assigned to the eighth table in the summer months, Europe will be obliterated at breakfast and Central Africa at lunch. But by supper, the whole world is magnificently restored in all its component parts. She trains her eyes on that part of the map which she supposes to signify the district where the school is, and then, widening her focus, she sees the province and then the country until her eye muscles slacken and relax and the world is floating before her – a wash of blurry colours; an unboundaried palette of territory on which you might live anywhere or nowhere.

She has not seen much of the world. She only really knows the school where she lives, Pim's farm, where she goes for exeats, and her own farm, where she spends three weeks in the spring, three weeks in the autumn and six weeks in the summer. And she doesn't even really know if she knows her own farm anymore.

She felt she knew it when she was very small. She knew it in senses – in smells (the musky lanolin of sheep's wool; the dustier odours of ostrich feathers), in colours (olive-green hills, her mother's face, pink and gentle under a blue headscarf), in sounds (the dry wind forcing the cabbage trees against the roof of the house, the winter crackle of grass under her feet) and in touch (the dainty shells of the pods from the Chinese Lantern bush that grew outside her window).

Then she came away, and her landscape became the more geometric vistas of the school, the squares of playing fields, the clean edges of buildings rising against a cyan sky. The smells were antiseptic – chalk dust; the smoke billowing from the kitchen furnaces. Her mother sent letters, but she couldn't read yet, and the year prefect read the children's letters aloud to them after supper, moving from bunk to bunk, but the others could hear anyway and she was afraid of the year prefect and her mother's words came out in the year prefect's voice. The weather went from hot to mild, and she learned to make letters into words and add up numbers and, at first, all the children cried into their pillows, but later it was quiet. Some of the boys in her class stoned a rabbit to death and got jacks, and she made a picture of the rabbit as it was when it was still alive in its cage behind the school block and got a star. The teacher said she had a heart of gold and the boys said she was a suck and all the boys were at war with all the girls for a bit. There was a man on the moon and some teachers thought it was progress, but some teachers thought it was a sin to challenge God.

One morning after breakfast her mother reappeared in her pink face and blue headscarf, speaking in her own voice. The dormitory was full of other mothers ransacking cupboards and packing suitcases which the groundsmen brought up from the cellar, because it was the holidays.

Holidays meant driving back to the farm, along the endlessly unfolding ribbon of highway with its blotches of grey dancing in the sun and the dun patches of stripped earth on either side. But when they got there it felt different and unfamiliar, and in the evening when her mother ran a bath and tried to undress her, Lally slapped her hands away.

She prefers Pim's farm, where she doesn't belong, to her own farm, where she doesn't belong either but has to sit at meals with her mother and father, the carriage clock ticking sonorously on the mantelpiece, all pretending they belong to each other, when in the end, you only ever belong to yourself.

The map of the world gives her a peculiarly pleasurable, almost physical sensation. It's not unlike the feeling, a few years back, when the children in the dormitory started to sneak across to each other's bunks, climbing between the sheets to lie pressed together; skin and hair and sweet toothpaste-scented breath, licking one another's eyelids with impossibly glad tongues – *do you love me, Mary? I love you, Sylvie* – the moon rising cold and remote in the un-curtained square of the window. They stopped collectively because someone got a book and there was, unhappily, a name for what seemed unnameable, and it was disconcerting to discover that they were lesbians.

The feeling-of-the-map has the same quality of invitation, an in-your-stomach anticipation as if it was pulling you toward something which, although you didn't know what it was, you knew you wanted it terribly. So, while the other children are lobbying for her unwanted spuds, Lally is shifting the map in and out of focus, savouring whatever it is that is more sublime than a potato.

Diversions

Television came to South Africa two years ago, which was a lot of years after overseas got it, because of Prime Minister Verwoerd not wanting to put the nation at risk. But no one in the town had one until the Mackenzies got one. Dr Mackenzie is an optician, and probably the richest man in town, since there are a lot of eyes but only one optician. He is also a Fabian socialist, which sounds dangerous but isn't. Dr Mackenzie has a surgery on the high street, but on Saturday mornings he goes into the township and looks at people's eyes for nothing. Sometimes he gives lectures on

Fabian socialism at the town hall. Dr Mackenzie believes that the white man came to Africa not only to govern and prosper, but also to protect.

Mrs Mackenzie, the doctor's wife, is Lally's history mistress. She's young and pretty and apple-cheeked, and she is always giggling, especially when anyone raises the subject of Dr Mackenzie. All the boys are silly over Mrs Mackenzie, which makes them rowdier than usual and more apt to ask impertinent questions.

'What's your first name, Mrs Mackenzie?'

'Boys!' admonishes Mrs Mackenzie, but after a moment she relents and says 'Elizabeth'.

'Does Dr Mackenzie call you Elizabeth?'

'Oh, really!' She's not going to answer that one.

'Does Dr Mackenzie call you Liz?' press the boys.

Mrs Mackenzie giggles so everyone knows that Dr Mackenzie calls her Liz, and soon half the desks on the boys' side of the classroom have 'Liz' carved into them.

Mrs Mackenzie describes the television and how it works, and everyone is desperate to see it for themselves. Mrs Mackenzie says the top three children in the history test can come to her house for supper and watch the news on television. This is a wily manoeuvre on Mrs Mackenzie's part because the boys who give her the most trouble are not likely to come top in the history test. In the end, Lally is selected and a plump, breathy girl they call Fat Betty and a nervous, underdeveloped boy whom the other boys call Zulu for a joke, because he isn't circumcised.

After supper, Fat Betty and Lally and Zulu gather at the top gates and walk to the Mackenzies' house on the northwestern edge of the town, which is the wealthiest part. Although they've got a permission slip, Fat Betty and Lally feel decadent because they aren't allowed to walk out of the grounds without an escort, especially not at night with a

boy, but it has all been achieved because crafty Mrs Mackenzie has buttered up the head of the girls' division by inviting
her to come over sometime to see the television herself.

The night is moonless and soft and, as they walk under the exaggerated stars, the hot unshifting air brushing
against their cheeks feels like rabbit pelts. On either side
of the street stand the tin houses, single-storeyed and spacious, with huge hopeful rain barrels resting on the roofs
from which skeins of purple and scarlet bougainvillaea spill.
The houses have verandas facing on to the street. Some of
the families are eating dinner on the verandas in circles of
light thrown out by hanging gas lamps, in whose more immediate halos the careless gnats fail to prepare themselves
for death.

The scents of flowers in the night air flow out, tremen-
dously potent, from the gardens – beds of roses and arcs
of wisteria over wrought-iron gates, and frangipanis dropping their perfumed petals as wantonly as handkerchiefs.
Some of the gardens are big enough for horses, and they
come crowding to the fence, their lashed, droopy eyes full
of greed, velvet lips tickling from the children's hands the
stolen sugar they fetch out of their pockets. Away from the
other boys, Zulu reveals himself to be surprisingly witty.
His rubbery face, if not so attractive in itself, is designed
for mimicry and he carries off the more brutal teachers and
prefects. It is good to laugh in the darkness at what is really
most frightening in the daylight.

Zulu is learning to play the violin and the piano, and also
the trombone. Playing the trombone is a secret strategy
because, when the other boys are having their balls busted,
Zulu will be in the Navy Band tootling away at tea parties
in the Western Cape for the entertainment of the prime
minister's wife.

Suddenly they are knocking at the door of the Mackenzies' house, which is a brick house, and Mrs Mackenzie is standing in a rectangle of light.

'Come inside,' she says, and she is even prettier in the world outside than she is at school. In the hallway behind her, there are personal things – paintings and photographs, a telephone with a message pad and a pencil tick-tacked to the wall behind it. The children feel clumsy in their uniforms and continue to stand awkwardly just outside the doorway, shuffling their feet.

'Hang up your blazers,' says Mrs Mackenzie, pointing to the rack, and once they're in their shirtsleeves it feels better. She leads them through to the living-room where Dr Mackenzie is resting in an armchair and watching the television. Dr Mackenzie is twenty-three years older than Mrs Mackenzie, which some people say is less than decent, and which makes him generally less exuberant than his wife.

'Oh! I wanted to see it from the beginning,' exclaims Fat Betty inadvertently, and puts her hand up to her mouth.

'It starts at six o'clock,' says Mrs Mackenzie.

'No – I meant the switching it on part.'

Obligingly, Dr Mackenzie switches it off and they all look at the television, which is a big square box with a front of black glass and a walnut exterior.

'Help me bring the snacks,' suggests Mrs Mackenzie, 'and then we'll watch the news.'

Zulu sits down on the sofa next to Dr Mackenzie while Mrs Mackenzie shepherds the girls through to the kitchen. She has made pâté and biscuits and baked little shiny sausage rolls. Fat Betty carries these things out on a tray whilst Lally and Mrs Mackenzie make the tea. You can tell Mrs Mackenzie is from the city originally because she makes tea by boiling up the water and adding a bag to the teapot right at the end, instead of letting the leaves steep and using a strainer.

When they come through from the kitchen, Fat Betty has taken the place next to Zulu on the sofa and Dr Mackenzie is saying that as far as he is concerned women teachers should be paid the same salary as male teachers for doing the same job.

'Darling,' intones Mrs Mackenzie softly because, although she feels strongly about the pay issue, it is not really an appropriate subject for the moment.

Fat Betty has been trying to get the outside edge of her hand to touch the side of Zulu's hand where it is lying on the sofa, without it seeming as if she did it on purpose. But when the tea arrives, it is all right to start with the snacks, and her attention is diverted. While the others begin to eat, Lally looks around the room – at the daisies on the print curtains, the marble fireplace, the pretty china dishes on the sideboard.

'Aren't you hungry, Laeticia?' asks the doctor.

'No thank you, Dr Mackenzie, we already had supper at the hostel.' That's an outright lie, and Fat Betty opens her crumb-specked mouth indignantly, because it's not at all fair to look as if you are stuffing your face when you are only eating dinner, but Lally gives her a flat look. Anyway, Dr Mackenzie is on his knees in front of the television now, fiddling with the controls. At first it is silent, and then there is a kind of low hum and suddenly a flash of blue light struggles into being in the middle of the black glass. It looks as if the black will win, but the blue is valiantly expanding and contracting and with a final bark of static, colours are filling the screen and voices are leaking into the room.

'I can get a clearer picture,' announces Dr Mackenzie professionally, squinting through his spectacles at the control panel, and for a few seconds the images are snowy, but then they jump back into focus. The news music plays as the news logo revolves. Next the headlines are up, and then the newsreader appears behind his desk, immaculately suited and very serious.

'How can he remember all the words?' marvels Fat Betty.

'He's reading,' explains Dr Mackenzie.

'But his eyes aren't moving.'

You can't put one over on Fat Betty. Dr Mackenzie tries to figure out how you can read without moving your eyes, but even with his specialist knowledge of the subject he is defeated. In Cape Town, the Navy has acquired a new ship. The ship is pulling out of port and on deck all the sailors in their spotless white uniforms are saluting.

'I'm going into the Navy,' says Zulu.

'It's not easy to get into the Navy,' Dr Mackenzie warns.

'Yes, but my brother is Permanent Force.'

'Oh, I see,' says Dr Mackenzie agreeably. 'Well, that should help.'

In Paris, the traffic has gridlocked. All the Parisian drivers are jumping out of their cars and shaking their fists. It is springtime in Paris – fat French women are leaning out over window boxes filled with geraniums, and languid boys and girls in jeans and jean jackets are sprawling on park benches watching the dyspeptic drivers. The camera pulls back in an aerial shot to show the extent of the gridlock – miles and miles of cars in a motionless radial spider-web clamped to the streets of the city.

Lally has been to two cities – Port Elizabeth and East London – but those are not cities in the sense that Paris is a city. Lally can't believe, firstly, just how enormously big Paris actually is, and secondly that it is possible to sit here in the Mackenzies' living room and look at the Parisians – real Parisians, who really were shaking their fists and leaning out of their windows only this morning.

The images of Paris give Lally the map-of-the-world feeling, only much more vigorously, so that she is suddenly as antsy as if it was the last chapel service before the holidays, and her breath is coming and going as if she has been running.

Inside her blouse, little shivers ripple up and down her back and chest and she sits back hard on her knees so that the heels of her shoes press reassuringly into her bottom. There is a sharp metallic taste in her mouth and her thighs, poking from beneath her tunic, are covered with goosebumps.

'We went to Paris on honeymoon,' says Dr Mackenzie.

'Oh, yes,' tinkles Mrs Mackenzie unguardedly. 'Do you remember that ridiculous little *pension*?'

She smiles at Dr Mackenzie, and it is startlingly apparent that no boy in Lally's class will ever have a snowball's chance in hell of getting Mrs Mackenzie, even once they have grown up. Zulu has got it bad thinking about Dr Mackenzie and Mrs Mackenzie and the ridiculous little *pension* in Paris, and he leans forward on his hands as if he had just come from jacks. Fat Betty is slowing down with the sausage rolls, and once more lets her own hand come to rest against Zulu's insubstantial trombonist's fingers.

Now there is the rugby and a death notice for a brave soldier who died fighting the communist enemy on the imperilled borders, with organ music in the background and the bronze statue of a *troepie* holding a rifle to remind viewers of those who are giving their lives for freedom and to stop Africa becoming a playground for Russia. 'God bless him,' says Mrs Mackenzie, but Lally is still having the Paris feeling.

On the way home, Fat Betty reveals that she has cigarettes – not only cigarettes, but the whole kit: matches, Clorets for their breath and Wet Wipes for their fingers. There is an empty lot with a thick, badly-maintained hedge, so they scramble through a hole in it and peel off their blazers, leaving a burgundy-and-black-striped hillock a few yards away in the dewy grass where the drift of the smoke won't curl into the wool. The cigarettes take a long time to burn down and bring the obsessed gnats hovering through the air. The tobacco makes Lally's head spin, but it also calms her.

Zulu stubs his cigarette out. He asks if he can kiss Fat Betty and Fat Betty asks why he doesn't want to kiss Lally. Zulu answers astutely that he doesn't think Lally wants to kiss him, and Fat Betty has an internal struggle over how she should take that remark, but in the end she asks Lally if she would mind, and Lally shakes her head. She sits tolerantly in the thick of the hedge whilst Zulu's tongue slides experimentally over Fat Betty's teeth and the inside of her cheeks, adding itself to the list of things that have navigated the interior of Fat Betty's mouth during the evening. Fat Betty lets Zulu have a feel of one of her breasts through the tunic as well, but when he tries to put his hand underneath the material she decides it's time to go home.

Back in the girls' division where everyone is preparing for lights out and the fags are at the range making hot chocolate for their fag mistresses, Lally takes the permission slip to the prefect to be signed off. When she gets back to the dormitory she notices Fat Betty is sitting cross-legged on the bed, her eyes dancing and a secret, luminous smile on her lips. Lally crosses over to her own bed and wriggles beneath the cover and the year prefect comes to put the light off.

But she can't sleep for the longest time because her mind is full of Paris; the drivers who waved their fists, the housewives who leant out of the windows. Across the room, Fat Betty is also restless, churning and twisting in the hot sheets, following through in fantasy what might have been if she had not made Zulu put his hand away and if Lally had not been there and if she had not been a Christian and going to be married in purity some day. When Fat Betty grinds in her bunk you can hear it, and after a while:

'Do be quiet, Betty,' complains Major Carlton's older daughter, who still cries out for her mother in her dreams.

'She's got a crush,' says Lally unkindly, and a handful of the girls snicker in the dark.

'Who is it? Who is it?'

Fat Betty is silent, waiting for the teasing to start in earnest, and Lally feels remorseful.

'No one,' she says, lying back on the pillow and, after a bit of badgering, the others lose interest and begin to fall asleep. There is some light feeding through from outside and Lally holds up her hands and presses the fingertips together. Up on the ceiling, the dim light flowing around the edges of her handshape makes a shadow just like the Eiffel tower.

Pont de la Tour

'I'll see you tomorrow, Mr Greenbow.'

'Oh, Laeticia,' Greenbow's slightly wobbling cheeks would clutch at her, but she's made it absolutely clear that she has to leave at five sharp today, and already she is filling in her hours on the timesheet.

She walks from the office to her bedsit, which is only a few streets away, past the signs of early summer in London – the slack alabaster stomachs of young girls in tank tops; the advertisements for holidays in Ibiza with their chi-chi suggestiveness.

Her bedsit is at the top of a once-elegant Edwardian house, and as she lets herself in she finds a gaggle of young people clustered on the stairs; mostly Australians but also another South African, or Zimbabwean, she guesses, from the way he goes about in flip-flops and shapeless khaki shorts. They are all in London on a Commonwealth work scheme and most of them are subsisting by making themselves available for medical experiments. They move from hospital to hospital, always hungry for work, never taking the required breaks, in a perpetual flurry of symptoms – eye-bags, trembling hands, throat thrush – from the flow of poisons cocktailing through their veins. Most of the time they are zoned out on alcohol and hash. One of the boys has had his big toe chopped off and sewn on again by trainee surgeons, and he's got his leg propped up on the banister in front of him, his foot marshmallowed in the plaster cast.

'Sorry,' she says, as he is barring her way.

'S'alright.' He thumps the foot down so that she can step over it.

As she goes up the stairs, she thinks that there must be more dignified ways to make a living. But then they probably don't think that being a thirty-five-year-old temporary secretary is the height of achievement.

Her room is simple – a desk and bed, the carpet ending where the kitchenette begins, a sink, a hot plate, a bar fridge which currently holds a bottle of Evian water and half an iceberg lettuce. The walls are covered with the sort of debris a discerning teenager might collect – flyers for the opera, a poem she liked in a magazine, a profile of Ralph Fiennes dressed up as Count Almásy. When it is time to go again, she will tear them from the walls and carry them out in a black bag to the side alley. Another black bag, another side alley, another city. With the instinct of a boarding school child or a traveller, she tries not to collect permanent things that have to be freighted about.

She strips off her secretarial skirt and jacket and opens the cupboard, passing her hand along the row of garments to see what texture she is in the mood for. In the end, she picks a pair of trousers in black velour and a dark green cotton T-shirt that fits snugly against her body. She brushes out her hair and paints her lips red, considering the effect in the mirror on the inside of the cupboard door. She was never thought pretty as a girl – too dark and lean and silent to stand out among those sashaying sagas of sunstruck limbs, those loud-voiced blonde voluptuaries who giggled behind their hands at school dances. But she is one of those women who became striking as she grew older, and she did, for a while, work as a catwalk model for lesser-known designers, flaunting the clothes which hung from her bird-wing shoulders.

She takes the Central Line to Bank and finds Pim's

building easily, waiting in the vestibule while the doorman calls him. Unknown armies of bankers are marching in and out of the glass-fronted edifice, and as they go past, talking tersely to each other or into their cellphones, they look at her surreptitiously. She knows she looks much younger than she is. She's never had children, never studied formally beyond school or had to pass exams, never had a significant job, never weathered a patch of depression without flying away from it. The lines of history are not as yet scoured across her face and her spare, boyish frame creates the illusion of perpetual adolescence.

Pim steps out of the lift between two other men. He is bigger than both of them, although she doesn't think of him as a big man. He is strongly built certainly – he was a formidable rugby player – but it is a more settled strength now, the younger man's rangy power replaced by the older man's certitude, and his blonde hair is greying along the temples.

He kisses her quickly on the cheek and steers her across the vestibule with a hand on her shoulder. They are outside on the pavement and Pim waves at a taxi and helps her inside, leaning forward to give the driver directions.

'London Bridge, please.' He settles back in the seat, and she can see from the distraction in his grey eyes that he is rehearsing what to say to her.

'I just thought it would be nice to have a drink peacefully,' he says 'and catch up. It's so difficult to have a real conversation with the children running around.'

The taxi driver asks: 'Which side of London Bridge?'

'South,' says Pim. 'Pont de la Tour. Do you know it?'

'Intimately,' says the taxi driver to his own eyebrows in the overhead mirror.

'I thought they were rather sweet,' says Lally, her remark helpful because it gives Pim the opportunity to be enthusiastic in return.

49

'Marvellous boys in every respect,' he agrees.

The traffic is heavy at this time. Pim tells Lally about a deal that is going through at the bank as they inch forward past the austere bulk of the Tower and over the Thames. When they get to the far side, he pays the driver and they go down the stone stairs to the restaurant. They sit at one of the outside tables where they can watch the river-boats ply up and down the visible stretch of water, and Pim orders champagne and chardonnay.

As she watches him she observes that he has become almost completely English. It shows in how he dresses and, most tellingly, in how he walks. He has lost the loose limbering swagger of the African boy she remembers and adopted a confined northern trot – as if he had grown up in a bitter climate; as if he really had learned to walk warding off the physical effects of cold.

He is filling in the bricks and mortar of his life for her since they lost touch. After the army and his first degree at the University of Cape Town, he was awarded the scholarship from their old school for boys to study at Oxford and he went up to do PPE. And after Oxford he moved to London.

There were some lovers and some adventures and some disappointments. Then there was Ruth and the boys. There are many anecdotes, and Lally has not heard any of them. Pim is a good raconteur, and Lally likes to listen. As she gets drunker, she watches his lips moving and the varying expressions behind his eyes.

'Edgar,' a voice behind them calls. Pim jumps slightly.

'Charlie,' he says. The new arrival, Charlie, is already a little drunk and he gives Lally a dry, appraising look and Pim an amused one.

'Lally is one of my oldest friends,' says Pim firmly to Charlie. 'Have a drink with us.'

'I don't want to *interrupt*.' Charlie has a submerged laugh threatening to come out.

'Oh, don't be ridiculous.' Pim's manner has become very sunny – perhaps even, Lally thinks, too sunny. Ebullient almost. She leans on her elbows and watches Pim and Charlie chuntering at each other. Yes, he has removed those parts of himself which are not English. And while he can't avoid admitting that he is, or was, South African, he has reinvented himself, creating the impression that he was one of those boys who attended select and austerely liberal private schools in Cape Town or Johannesburg and went on to Eton and Oxbridge as a matter of course and family tradition. It is clear that he does not want to be the rural boy he was. He refers to the farm off-handedly as 'our piece of land', as if it was something extraneous to the spirit of the family he was born into; as if it were not the complete obsession of five dead Pims and one live one; as if it were not his rejected birthright. And yet she still sees in his eyes the obscure hungerings and agonies of the exile.

It is really quite difficult to know what to do about Charlie. Pim and Lally drink steadily and rapidly. Charlie announces abruptly, 'Oh God – the time!' and vacates, leaving Lally and Pim trying to focus on each other.

'What is the time?' asks Lally.

'Just before eight.' He twitches his shirt cuff back from his wristwatch.

'When have you got to be back?'

'Eleven-ish.' He's still contemplating the watch, although its more obvious purposes are spent. 'If I'm working late.'

'You better sober up before then.'

'Yes.' He frowns at her. 'I should have eaten. We should get something.' He remembers her eating habits. 'Little salad or something.'

'Do they do take-outs?'

'Take-outs? At Pont de la Tour?' He shifts around in his chair, getting a gander at the dark-suited men and the women in their fitted dresses and groomed hair, the busy purse-mouthed waiters and the Jamaican attendant lingering in the doorway to the women's toilet. 'I shouldn't imagine they would.'

'Why don't we pick up a pizza?' she suggests. 'And I can show you where I live. It's not far from you.'

Life, which had seemed so muddily complicated a few minutes ago, suddenly reveals itself to Pim as being extraordinarily clear.

'OK,' he agrees, 'since it's on the way.'

He gets the bill and they stand up and walk carefully back up the stone steps.

Doubt

She understands nothing.

If she understands anything at all, it is only that she understands nothing.

She doubts everything.

If this doubt was a long time in building, it became clear to her rapidly – through three incidents – and each of these incidents was physical in its nature.

Because of this physicality, in later life, when she remembers the period of confusion, she remembers with her body more than her mind.

First

In the boys' division, a prefect discovers two boys touching each other in the showers after lights out. If they were small boys they might have got away with jacks, but they are not; one is a matric and the other is in Lally's class. In any case, the prefect marches them directly to the hostel master and by midnight the hostel master has called the headmaster and by breakfast all the boys' division knows about it and by afternoon all the girls' division as well. The two boys are to be expelled. Being expelled is the most terrible punishment imaginable, because it goes on your record with the reasons why, and afterwards only the lowest schools will have you and for the rest of your life your friends will be railwaymen and factory workers.

The matric boy goes to the headmaster and says that he made Shuttleworth, the boy in Lally's class, do it. He seduced Shuttleworth with many arguments, by constant persuasion, although for a long time Shuttleworth refused. In the end, it is decided to allow Shuttleworth to stay; to give him a second chance. A minister – who has had previous success in treating homosexuals – is to come from the city at weekends to help him. Shuttleworth signs a paper prepared by the minister, which is a contract with God for forgiveness and a promise that he will never seek to have contact of any kind with the older boy.

When children are to be expelled, they are placed in the sanatorium until their transport arrives. When the matric boy is expelled, there are five days to go until the train for his home town is due. The sanatorium is a low-slung building which lies between the school block and the sports fields, and the children have occasion to pass it several times a day. While the boy is in there, the building holds a kind of fascination – an aura of scandal – and they drag their feet on the way to practice and their dormitories, trying to catch a glimpse inside. But he keeps away from the windows.

Meanwhile Shuttleworth has gone back to class, after two days' absence. The odd thing about Shuttleworth is that you would not have placed him for a poofter: he is strong and sinewy with lively white-blonde hair that grows so quickly it has to be cropped once a fortnight. He plays for the under sixteens, and his mates are all from the team.

Shuttleworth arrives for the first lesson of the morning after the siren has already gone and everyone is in their desks. He stops in the doorway and hesitates, because a situation has arisen. The children change classrooms for every lesson, but they always keep their place at a regular desk. Now Shuttleworth sees that there has been a shifting of seats and that the only free desk is on the extreme edge of the boys' half, at the front of the classroom, almost in the girls' half. He hitches his schoolbag further up on his shoulder and looks over at the desk, an abstracted expression on his face, as if he was trying to remember something or counting numbers in his head. He moves down the aisle and takes his seat.

The master is drawing a parabola on the board. But the twinned arcs of Shuttleworth's shoulders bending over his desk are more interesting by far. Two of Shuttleworth's friends from his old position at the back of the classroom have started taking the mickey. They are pursing their lips at each other and making muted groans, fluttering their hands in limp-wristed and ostentatious gestures.

'Forster!' says the master sharply, looking up. 'Van Niekerk!'

The boys subside, but there is a giggle going round the classroom – a giggle like a passed note – so that every few minutes someone will catch it and snort breathily over their work. The giggle is because of the new nickname Shuttleworth has got, which he doesn't yet know about – Shafter Shuttleworth. Shuttleworth's ears have darkened – are purple, almost – but his whole attention seems occupied with copying down the parabola and the obscurities which the master is scribbling underneath it.

Toward the end of lessons, the more energetic children are given to sliding their workbooks into their schoolbags and crouching like hares behind their desks, so that when the siren goes they can spring out into the corridors and roughhouse with each other for a few minutes before the next class. Those, like Lally, who suffer from shyness, have a stratagem which minimises the period of their exposure in the boisterous corridors. They put all manner of objects on their desks – pens and pencils, compasses, notebooks

– that have to be individually packed away at the sound of the siren. And now when Lally looks up she sees that Shuttleworth, who only days ago was a scuffler and a teaser himself, is opening up his pencil case –uselessly extracting and lining up a sharpener, an eraser, a ballpoint – a battalion of distractions marching inexorably towards the abyss of the inkwell.

She never sleeps well, and one night, later in the week, she finds she can't sleep at all. She climbs out of her bunk and kneels in her nightgown at the window. She stares at the quarter moon until she feels as contained as moon rock herself and listens to the fervent cricket orchestras in the heath embankments. Some heavy vehicle bringing produce into the town gears down on the incline of the valley hill and, against this noise, the whispering crunch of cautious bare feet on gravel draws her attention. A figure in pyjamas is tiptoeing over the gravel yard in front of the boys' division. As soon as he can he makes a flying leap for the grass and lands cat-like on his feet, slipping noiselessly across the verges towards the sanatorium. She sees him freeze against the brick face of the building as the careless headlights of a car passing on the public road rake across the lawns. He waits for a minute or two – peering through the gloom – not towards her, but back in the direction of the boys' division. At last, he starts to edge around the corner of the building, stepping with the deliberate nervousness of some stilt-legged water bird – until he reaches the window that has captivated them all these past few days. He checks left and right, and taps softly against the pane.

The boy comes to the window. She can see the pale round shape of his face, but his features are unclear. Shuttleworth presses himself to the barrier between them, his two hands spanned flat against the glass. He is speaking and the boy behind the glass is answering. For five minutes or so he remains in that attitude, his head turning left and right intermittently like an over-cautious pedestrian who is never to cross the road. At last, she detects in Shuttleworth's shoulders that whatever words must pass between them are spent, and he is preparing to go. He moves back and the outline of the older boy is more visible now.

This private room in the sanatorium is designed for children who are to be expelled or have tried to run away, and the windows do not open. But at the top of the sealed window is a small ventilation window on a catch. The shadowy form behind the glass reaches up and slides his hand over the ledge as far as the aperture will permit. The pyjama sleeve slips down Shuttleworth's arm as he echoes the movement. And as she watches, Lally's own fingers are closing hard against each other in the pocket of her nightgown.

Second

A relative of Zulu's who has been on business to Singapore has sent him a box of firecrackers. The firecrackers are twists of gunpowder the size of a marble. They come in red-and-white striped paper wrappers with pictures of Chinese-looking dragons and Chinese letters on them. If you throw them hard at the ground they explode with a bang, leaving the tart smoky stink of gunpowder lingering on the air. Although they don't always work.

But the one Zulu throws at Fat Betty's feet just before the English lesson works brilliantly. It is winter now, and it's seven thirty in the morning. Fat Betty is in her gloves and scarf. When the blast goes off, she screams, pulling her gloved hands out of her blazer pockets and putting them over her ears, staring wildly around her for the origin of the noise.

It's even funnier because lately everyone has been thinking about bombs. The terrorists have been exploding bombs, and they don't mind where they do it. They blow up post offices and supermarkets. In the cities, some of the supermarkets make you walk through a doorway-like machine similar to the one at the airport. A policeman comes to the school to give a lecture on bombs and bomb awareness. If you see any suspicious parcel you can't identify you should give it a wide berth and call an expert immediately. And you should never ride your bicycle over an empty box lying in the street. At the as-yet-intact post office on the high street, there is a three-dimensional placard which shows the actual shape of all the different kinds of bombs that the African National Congress uses to conduct its campaign of terror.

So, when Zulu throws the firecracker at Fat Betty, she thinks at first that it is a terrorist attack and everyone has a laugh. Fat Betty says 'Oh, you are a pest!' to Zulu, but she's over the shock already and she's even quite pleased, because a certain kind of teasing from a boy can really be disguised affection.

The siren for the first lesson starts to wail, crisp and distinct in the chilly air, and the children hurry inside from the front yard. Because everyone has to study English, the year is divided into several streams. Fat Betty and Lally and Zulu are in the top stream. The top stream gets the best teacher, who is Mr Payne. Mr Payne is the best teacher in that he has a master's degree as well as an ordinary teaching certificate, but he is not necessarily the best teacher in other ways. If you give him a wrong answer he repeats it in a voice that makes it sound silly as well as ignorant. And he makes the other children laugh at you.

Mr Payne tells everyone to open their poetry books to 'The Unknown Citizen' by WH Auden. He tells the class that 'The Unknown Citizen' is a poem about living in a community. Another way in which Mr Payne is not the best teacher is that he is not very interesting, and it is hard to keep track of what he is saying. Lally finds herself looking out of the window into the winter morning, at the fluffed-up curmudgeonly hadedas making greatcoats out of their feathers and scraping at the frost-hardened ground with their beaks. A groundsman outside is pushing a wheelbarrow full of tins of paint. His loose overalls are already stained with paint and there are even some pale green streaks on his balaclava and his gumboots. He puts down the wheelbarrow and rolls himself a cigarette; his thick labourer's fingers tubing up the paper more quickly than you would think possible. He uses Boxer – the coarse, cheap tobacco that the Africans buy. The smoke billows strongly in the winter morning. When another grounds-man trundles past with a wheelbarrow of his own, they call back and forth in rough, grunting voices; years of Boxer gurgling away at the back of their throats.

Mr Payne's nasal voice interrupts her observation.

'What is the poet calling for, Laeticia?'

'Individual recognition, Sir.' She never really listens, but she does subconsciously register and briefly store his running commentary. And he said 'individual recognition' a few seconds ago. They never quiz you further back than that.

There is a trio of boys who sit along the wall on the boys' side called Preston, McGrath and Bowyer. They are all-rounders – good at sport and lessons, and with a sporting attitude towards life.

Preston, McGrath and Bowyer have sturdy physiques and square-jawed, attractive faces with good teeth. They are always quick with answers, and sometimes they even have a bit of a laugh with the teachers in a respectful way.

McGrath puts his hand up. 'Sir?'

'Yes?'

'I think Auden is saying that we shouldn't have to wear school uniforms, Sir.'

'Hah! That would suit you down to the ground, wouldn't it, McGrath? Be an excuse not to sport your amazing lack of tin!'

That's meant as a joke, because McGrath has lots of tin actually, especially considering that he is only in Standard Eight. Tin is an amusing word for the badges on your blazer lapels. Mr Payne isn't put out by McGrath's witticism – teachers like Preston, McGrath and Bowyer because of their sporting attitude and because they are a credit.

Problems crop up with the part of the poem that goes:

He was married and added five children to the population, which our eugenist says was the right number for a parent of his generation.

A girl in the front row puts up her hand and says she doesn't understand the word 'eugenist'. Mr Payne writes 'EUGENICS' on the blackboard in yellow chalk. He launches into an explanation.

Lally notices that Preston has leant forward, put his hand into the pocket of Zulu's blazer where it is hanging on the back of the chair and extricated the box of firecrackers. He eases up the cardboard lid and takes out one of the crackers. Then he closes the box and slips it back into the blazer pocket. Zulu hasn't noticed because he sits directly in front of Preston, but most of the girls have, because they cut their eyes at Preston every few seconds anyway. An excitement comes into the classroom.

Mr Payne has got sidetracked into a discussion of why

two brown-eyed parents cannot produce a blue-eyed child. He is drawing a little diagram in order to illustrate the more confusing tenets of his argument when the firecracker detonates against the blackboard.

Commendably, but unfortunately for him in the current situation, Mr Payne is very much alive to the national bomb threat.

'GET DOWN!' he bawls, dropping to the floor in a textbook manoeuvre that is an almost exact copy of the body-flattening technique that the bomb expert taught them in assembly. Those who don't know about the Singaporean crackers are also hunkering on the floor below their seats, although by and large less adroitly than Mr Payne, and even the groundsman has come out of his long smoker's trance and is staring at the classroom window. But those still remaining in their desks are gripped by silent spasms.

Mr Payne stands up slowly with the spent cracker in his hand. His pinched, whitened nostrils make his face ugly, but not as ugly as his voice when he says:

'Who threw this?'

Nobody answers. The hairs that Mr Payne combs over the bald place at the back of his head have gone all awry.

'Right.' He has come to his senses and is moving quickly.

'Stand up and hands in the air, everyone. NOW!'

They all jump up and do as he says; their faces blank of expression. They look like twenty-three undersized war criminals surrendering.

'Kitty,' says Mr Payne, selecting a small timid girl who would be more likely to sprout wings and fly than to throw a firecracker. 'Collect the blazers.'

He has her put the boys' blazers on the left of the teacher's platform and the girls' blazers on the right. He starts searching through the boys' blazers first. There are several diversions.

'What is this, Barrington?'

'Chewing gum, Sir.'

'Is chewing gum allowed?'

'No, Sir.'

But at last he is holding the box of firecrackers in his hand. He turns it over so that he can have a look at both sides of it. He opens the pretty patterned lid and stirs his finger through the contents. No one says anything at all, but eyes are sliding towards Zulu. Mr Payne closes the lid of the firecracker box. He turns the collar of the blazer towards him so that he can see the name.

'Everyone sit.' And as the bottoms are halfway to the seats: 'Welford, remain standing.'

Welford is Zulu's real name. There is a sheen of sweat on Zulu's upper lip, and his narrow boy's chest is visibly expanding and contracting.

'Welford, did you bring explosives into the classroom?'

The question takes everyone by surprise. Zulu had been gearing up for denial, but now he remains silent, biting on his lip, his eyes moving between Mr Payne and the firecrackers.

'*Did … you … bring … explosives … into … the … classroom?*'

The word 'explosives' sounds volatile and dangerous in the silence of the room. A pleading look comes into Zulu's face.

'They're firecrackers, Sir. And I didn't …'

'Do you *know*, do you have any *idea*, of the kind of injuries these devices can cause?'

'No, Sir,' says Zulu miserably.

'You're an idiot,' says the master. 'Come to the front. Kitty, give everyone back their blazers.'

Kitty restores the blazers to their owners while Mr Payne writes Zulu an order slip for jacks. The classroom is still very quiet. They are all watching the dance of Mr Payne's ballpoint pen on the order slip. Zulu has his back turned to the rest of the class. Lally is struggling. She wants to tell Mr Payne that it wasn't Zulu who threw the firecracker, but she feels she can't. She doesn't even know who did throw it. At least, she knows it was Preston, McGrath and Bowyer, but she doesn't know which one. She saw Preston steal the cracker, but Bowyer bowls for the first side in cricket and has the best aim. And anyway, Mr Payne seems more concerned with the fact that the crackers were in the classroom in the first place than the incident of someone having thrown one at the blackboard.

Zulu leaves the room. His shoulders are bent and he is lifting his legs with a heavy deliberation as if there were burdensome weights on his shoes. Mr Payne is already carrying on with the poem as if nothing had happened. A hard, critical feeling wells up in Lally towards Mr Payne. She considers that he has cheated by shifting his ground. He took the easiest option because he can't know for definite who threw the cracker, but he could establish who owned them.

She looks over at Fat Betty. Fat Betty is jack-knifed over 'The Unknown Citizen' as if her life depended on getting it off by heart by the end of the lesson. She glances up when she feels Lally's eyes on her, but returns her gaze instantly back to the anthology, setting her shoulders fractionally against Lally. On the other side of the classroom, Preston, McGrath and Bowyer are hard at their books, but Bowyer's dimples are sunk more deeply into his cheeks than usual and there is a mirthful fixity about the way McGrath's excellent teeth are closing on his pen.

A hot, dirty feeling splashes over Lally as if someone had poured a bucket of urine on her head. It is shame. She will never stand up for Zulu, and neither will Fat Betty or anyone else, because they are all scared. They are scared of the all-rounders Preston, McGrath and Bowyer. The teachers are on their side and one day they will be prefects for sure, and when they grow up they'll be officers and mayors and police brigadiers and parliamentarians. And Zulu is nothing but a skinny little trombonist. If you get on the wrong side of Preston, McGrath and Bowyer it will come back at you forever and ever. But if Zulu hates everybody else in the class, it is nothing.

Towards the end of the lesson there is a rap on the door. Mr Payne says: 'Enter.' Zulu comes in, holding the cloth of his trousers away from his backside. He gives the signed order slip to the master and eases himself painstakingly into his desk. Lally tries to catch his eye, but he isn't looking at the other children: he's looking straight ahead.

Zulu hasn't grown properly. He doesn't shave – not even once a month – and his voice is as fluting as a dove's. But there is a look on his face now – a defeated look; a look of resignation – and it frightens Lally because it seems unnatural for someone as puny and under-grown as Zulu to wear an old man's face.

Third

A few hours after the English lesson, in the middle of the morning, a panic comes over her. It is the time when the children have tea and jam sandwiches on the verandas of their divisions. The panic is a clawing, physical thing. It makes her heart hammer in her chest and brings a metal taste into her mouth. She sucks at the air to get enough of it and feels she will choke. The milling, noisy children make it worse. Although she is not allowed into the dormitories during lessons, she runs upstairs to her bunk.

Upstairs it is quieter and therefore a little better, but she cannot rid her head of these two images: the pyramid of the lovers' hands at the window; the old-man face that Zulu wore. They click in her inner vision as if she were peering into one of those slide machines that children are given to see Disney pictures, and she is unable to push them away.

The door swings open and she jerks her head up thinking it must be a prefect, but it is only the sisi come to empty the wastepaper baskets and wipe the basins clean. She stares down at the bed again. The sisi is plump in pale-blue overalls and a white doek. She wears socks and battered tennis shoes and, as she wipes and tips the bins into her black bag, she hums a ditty to herself. With the sisi in the room, Lally's panic subsides some more. She stares down at her duvet with its alternating red-and-blue diamond shapes. The diamonds are weirdly distinct against the cotton. It is as if there are strange out-of-control chemicals pouring through her veins. She forces herself not to concentrate on the images. She tries to follow mentally the mundane tasks with which the sisi is busy.

Unexpectedly, the woman walks over towards her bed, sits down on it and puts both her arms around Lally. Lally is shocked. It is in her mind to struggle – to pull herself away from the woman's African-woodsmoke smell, mixed with the odours of Brasso and Jik – when she realises that she is crying. Not even just crying; bawling – as if she were a child, like she used to cry in her mother's arms over some accident or disappointment before she came away to school. The sisi's overall front is quickly smeared with mucus and tears, but she continues to rock Lally and sing the ditty. Lally doesn't speak Xhosa – they don't learn it at school, and the workers on her parents' farm are Afrikaans-speaking coloureds – but the words of the song seem to be reassuring. She tries to explain to the sisi. 'It's about Shuttleworth. Zulu didn't throw the cracker,' but that's silly, because the sisi doesn't know about any of that. And she is embarrassed that she is crying over these things because the black people have problems of the most daunting nature – the little urchins in town bending their arms against their stomachs and holding out their grimy hands for coins; the women going door-to-door with strained, drawn faces, asking to be allowed to do the washing.

The siren goes for the end of tea. The sisi reaches over to the top of Lally's locker, takes a handful of tissues from a tissue box, wipes Lally's face then holds the tissue to her nose to blow. Lally submits. The sisi stands, puts the tissue in her black bag with the other wastepaper basket rubbish, and leaves the room. Lally breathes in and out slowly a few times before she also stands.

When she gets downstairs, the walkways to the school block are already almost empty and she has to trot in order not to be late. She feels still now – emotionally still – with a drugged, post-weeping calm. She sits drowsily through the classes; slack as a scarecrow in the desk, propped up on her arms in their burgundy jumper sleeves.

Sisi

Her name is Sisi between seven in the morning and five in the afternoon on weekdays, also on her one weekend shift per month. At other times she is Nomda to her friends and her mother; Mama to her two daughters and her son.

She was born on a farm not far from the town. She married a man and went to the Transkei to live with his family. He went to the mines and, at first, came back every year and gave her a child, but later he never came back. She heard that he had a woman there at the mines. He still sent money sometimes, but the money went to his mother and did not come through his mother to Nomda. She quarrelled with her mother-in-law, who was imperious and unkind. Eventually she went back with her children to her birth-farm and her own mother, and worked as a housemaid for the *oumiesies* there. When the *baas* died, relatives came to fetch the *oumiesies* and the farm was sold. The new *miesies*, who did not for some reason approve of her, chose other housemaids. So Nomda came to the town with her children and her mother. They have a shack in the township, and they all live off her cleaner's salary. They eat *phutu*, sometimes with chicken or goat, or goat entrails if money is short. When the children are sick, Nomda goes into the veld for herbs, as her mother did before her.

Coming into the room she sees the child sitting cross-legged on the bed. She has been working in this cleaning job for ten years, but she does not like the white children. She does not like their hard-angled bodies and their stony, guarded faces. They order her about in sharp, important little voices in a way that makes her indignant. When they are almost grown, like this one, they practise on her for the madams they will soon become. Mostly they pay her no attention at all, airing their secrets in front of her as if she were a brick or a piece of furniture while she picks up their things.

But sometimes she finds herself stretching towards the more obviously wounded. This child on the bed she has seen on several occasions sitting like this, as still as a *klipspringer* trying to smell out a leopard, and with the same attitude of alert attention, her pale arms strait-jacketed around her scrawny waist.

She does not understand the white people. They seem to have no organ of emotion in them. No, that is too simple – they have emotions, but they stifle them. It is a virtue with them. Even when the *baas* died and the black women were keening outside the church, the white women, the *baas*'s own wife and daughter, sat like rocks in their pews. There is a connection in her mind between white people and rocks. She sees it in the children. When they are young they are like puppies, and as they grow older they become like stones.

The area in which the whites are hardest to understand is in their attitude towards children. They do not love their children. They love only what is useful in their children. That is why they send them away so young – to the lines of beds, to the queues, to the lessons – to encourage what is useful and to eliminate what is not useful.

At the same time, she recognises that this control of emotion is their greatest strength in rule. It is what allows a handful of them to dominate the whole mass of her people. It allows them to think together and act together, without regret. A purposeful herd beyond the sum of its parts. And it is the most frightening thing about them. If they can free themselves from the heart-clutch of their own children, how much more will they do to her people, with whom they have no bond?

If the whites have no emotion, sometimes she thinks her own people are rotten with it – sliding always between anger and laughter and tears. Even now, she is annoyed with herself for bleeding in her heart towards this statue of a child on the bed. There is no reason to feel sympathetic. In external things, the lives of the white children are easy. She is already looking for a position for her own eldest daughter, who is the same age.

Tonight, she will go home and she will cook an iron pot of *phutu* on the brazier behind the shack, with cabbage and with spinach. She will carry the pot inside and give a plate to her old mother, who will sit upright in the bed with her enormous old woman's legs stretched out straight, telling some wandering old woman's story while her granddaughters giggle on the end of the bed, braiding each other's hair, their plump Vaselined limbs glowing like mahogany in the candlelight. The boy will come in from playing soccer with his friends. Their team is the Fingo Pirates. They don't have money for strips, but they wear what they have in red-and-blue and write big numbers in indelible marker on squares of a torn-up sheet that they pin to their backs with safety-pins. He will come in and spoon his dinner rapidly into his mouth. However much there is to eat, he will still be hungry. He is that age. His hands and feet too big for his body, his voice uncertain and stammering sometimes between a high and low pitch, which makes him shy. Although he is also cocky, despite the stammering and the gangly all-over-flopping limbs. The sisters like to laugh and tease him. He is losing his milk-sweet child smell and getting a man-sweat smell when he plays hard games outside in the dust. The sisters hold their noses with pinched thumb and forefinger and wave the other hand below. She has to get cross with the teasing. She says '*Hayi suka thula wena – stop it*!' to the girls, who are over early puberty and were, anyway, in a house of women when it happened. But the boy seems not to mind. He is not like his father, who went away and never came back – he likes to be in all the business of family life; looking in the supper pot and giving her advice about the quantities of meat to add (always more) and spinach (always less). The sisters tease again – *hey, big man, go out and bring home the meat.*

Tonight, there will be the teasing, the cocky-shy blustering of the boy, the old mother's stories. But this white child will lie down in her bunk, rigidly, as she is now sitting rigidly on top of it.

There are many things Nomda regrets about her life. She wishes always that there was more money. She wishes that her husband had not disappeared. There were other things that seemed terrible at the time which, in retrospect, were better for her and for her family. Like the *baas* dying and having to leave the farm, for example. So many things have happened and there have been many different feelings occasioned by those circumstances.

But one feeling that she has not had, except for the time with her mother-in-law when the children were too young to be company, is the feeling of loneliness.

She crosses the room and she puts her arms around the white child.

Decision

For some weeks after these incidents, Lally is filled with doubt, the way a sponge fills with water. The whole shape of her soul is connected to the doubt. There are a thousand murmuring voices streaming like a rain torrent through her mind. The voices of adults, teachers, newspapers are incanting, intoning, chanting all the opinions, advice, perorations she has ever heard. On and on, with a static, endless quality. Even her dreams, usually vivid and visual, are now a blank, black panel across which the voices whisper and chase.

The voices reverberate against the three images; the pyramid of lovers' hands at the window, the old-man face of Zulu, the sisi's arms.

One night she falls asleep and wakes several hours later, becoming sharply and simultaneously aware that the voices have gone away and that a change has taken place.

She has arrived at an understanding.

She has been living in a delusionary world.

Realising this does not make her hysterical. In fact, she has never felt calmer. It is as if she had stepped into an enormous hollow block of ice and the walls of ice had sealed behind her. After the first shock of adjustment it is easy to see that the ice chamber has clear advantages. She is shut away from all the hot fluster of the world beyond and there is an icy, contained stillness in her curious new abode that makes it easier to think.

She thinks of Shuttleworth and his lover. It seems extraordinary to her that Shuttleworth's lover courted the wrath of the whole universe to keep Shuttleworth from being expelled. She has never protected anyone like that and she very much doubts that anyone will ever protect her like that. *Sex outside marriage is a terrible sin and homosexuality is the worst sin, more unnatural even than sleeping with a black.* She watches Shuttleworth's face in class to see if he is different for having been loved more selflessly than any of them.

Then there is the sisi. *The savagery of the black people lies in their capriciousness. They will work forty years faithfully for a single master and one day they will turn and stab him in the back.* After the day of the panic, she catches glimpses of the sisi shuffling around the dormitories in her worn tennis shoes. The sisi's flat, broadened facial features are usually composed into an expression of neutral calm that Lally finds encouraging.

She wants to give the sisi something, but she doesn't want to embarrass her. There is a blouse hanging in the cupboard – a present from her mother in the new fashion, yellow paisley shapes on brown satin. Lally presses the blouse on the sisi, who accepts it matter-of-factly.

'Aren't you too fat?' asks Lally artlessly, because whatever gift she gives won't express what it is meant to.

'My daughter will like it,' says the sisi, unoffended.

No, the sisi is not a savage. But Mr Payne, who masked his humiliation by picking on Zulu, is a savage. And Preston, McGrath and Bowyer of the sly, wide smiles are all definitely savages.

The ice chamber could also be described as a warehouse of truths. If, as yet, she knows only a few true things, it does not matter. The more true things she arrives at, the easier it will be to realise and pick them out.

She would like to keep a notebook where she could write down a taxonomy of true things, but she is afraid it will fall into the wrong hands. Also, the truths that seem so shattering in her head do not condense well into the solid forms of written words. Trapped inside the shell of letters, the truths seem puny and childlike; their vastness compromised.

It does not matter. Life, which seemed so sluggish and aimless, is now imbued with the feverish haste of the search for true things. She searches everywhere – in books, in newspapers, in conversations and lessons – trying to prise apart the layers of the false things so that the teachers shift their gaze from her disconcertingly attentive dark eyes.

The search for true things is a solitary pursuit. It does not occur to her to encompass anybody else. Anyway, nobody she knows seems to suspect the extent of the delusion, and there is a simple way of determining that they do not. Because the delusion is so great, if you want to be able to think about it at all you have to employ the most open kind of cognisant language. The width and breadth and height of the delusion cripples the sensible everyday language. In the face of the delusion, you have to be humble about language. All you can say is *this is not the way this is* and *this is other than it seems.*

The people she knows are always jabbering, but they jabber in the everyday language. One of the truths she has realised is that if you speak in a certain manner, you think in that manner too. You don't shape your words; they shape you. A searcher after truth has to keep language as general as possible. Everybody she meets uses a very specific language. So, there can't be other searchers after the truth.

And then one day something happens which makes her suspect that there might, after all, be at least one other searcher after the truth. And the suspicion arises from the most unexpected quarter.

A peculiar letter

Emily has had a letter from Pim. Pim is fighting the enemy, but he is not allowed to say where he is fighting them. The letter is a most extraordinary document, and not only because it comes from nowhere. Actually, it's not even a letter; it's a postcard. Emily, perhaps unwisely, reads it aloud to the girl from the Copper Belt at the top of the prefects' stairs in a high-pitched delivery, punctuated by sobs.

Dear Em

I'm coming home in a few weeks but I don't think we should see one another, or that you should visit. You will think it is the same, and it isn't – it's different. Or it never was what I thought it was. It was always something else.

I'm sorry.

Pim

'What's it about?' The stupefying letter is shaking in Emily's grip. 'What does it *mean*?'

But if Emily is dumbfounded, so is the girl from the Copper Belt and the forty unofficial pairs of ears in the cubicles below. Even when Lally, who ought to know Pim if anyone does, is summoned, she can shed no light on the letter. When Emily reads it, Lally's mouth falls open and her dark eyes lock uncomprehendingly on to Emily's face.

'I know,' groans Emily. She paces back and forth across the carpet, her pretty, symmetrical features scrunched up, knocking together the knuckles of her tanned, tennis player's hands.

'He must have met someone else. But who? There aren't any women up there except …'

Her hand flies to her mouth as the thought occurs.

'Oh, he wouldn't,' says the girl from the Copper Belt comfortingly, but she can't help glancing at the daughter of the diamond mining engineer. A man who could write such a strange letter might be lunatic enough to do anything. 'Perhaps it's shellshock,' says the mining engineer's daughter.

'*Shellshock?*' exclaims Emily. Shellshock seems to have little to do with how handsome Pim looked in his uniform, with the silver star on his shoulder.

The mining engineer's daughter considers. Shellshock does sound silly, and antiquated besides.

'Bush shock?' she suggests. But Emily's grim lips are not having truck with shocks of any kind. Noticing Lally still standing motionless on the carpet, she realises that Lally is a peculiar, silent and unlovely child who should not be in the prefectural annexe in the first place.

'Get out, Lally,' says Emily.

Pim, who was always popular, falls rapidly in the polls – the object of indignation from the prefects and of subdued annoyance from everyone else, because a prefect in a strop is a prefect looking for an outlet. Indeed, by the end of the day, Emily's order booklet has thinned considerably, and two juniors caught hopscotching five minutes into rest have got an afternoon detention.

At prayers, she catches a girl whispering and eyeing her. The girl is one of those skulking and insubordinate brigands – the non-prefect seniors. Emily orders the girl to come to her room after supper and, backed up by the silent support of the girl from the Copper Belt, who pretends to write a letter at the bureau, strips her of that perpetual boarding school Sword of Damocles – the Saturday morning leave-out.

'If it makes you feel better,' the girl shrugs. She was in dormitories for seven or eight years with these people before they were appointed, and she's underwhelmed by the chain of command.

Emily glowers. She would like to increase the punishment but she can't go above a leave-out without applying to a teacher, and she prefers her particular rung on the ladder to be a kingdom unto itself. The girl is slouching on the carpet, amid the detritus of the hierarchy with nothing to gain and nothing to lose that she cares about very much any more. In their very abjectness, the skulkers have a power which is infuriating. The girl knows that Emily's been pipped and the unironed hang of her blazer, the thrust of her hands in her pockets, the concertina'd wrinkle of her stockings all speak derision.

'Get out,' says Emily, and the skulker slopes off, down towards the skulker cubicles on the west face of the building. Skulkers still have certain privileges; they are all studying for the same national examination, skulkers and prefects alike, and the skulkers can put out their own lights when they put their books away. Late in the night when Emily goes down to use the ablutions, she can hear laughter coming unchecked from the skulker cubicles.

The memory of the laughter keeps her awake. She feels petulant and distressed. She tries not to think about Pim, which makes her think about him more. She remembers the first time he kissed her at a school dance, and a day or two afterwards when he ran to catch her up on the walkway and asked her if she wanted to go steady. It's hard to put away the crystal-clear, much-elaborated mental picture of how she was going to look on their wedding day, the yellow roses in her hair that were to match Pim's cummerbund. She forces her mind from the image. There is a dance coming up. Now that she is free, all the boys in her class will try to get her to go with them. But how can she go out with a schoolboy after an officer? She drizzles into the pillow. She will go anyway and have a damn good time and tell Lally all about it and then Lally will tell Pim and then Pim will be jealous. Will Pim be jealous? Oh, what's wrong with Pim! Her tears make a wide slobbery stain on the cotton pillowslip.

Downstairs in the Standard Eight dormitories, Lally is also awake and also thinking of Pim. *It never was what I thought it was. It was always something else.* Is it possible that Pim knows? A picture comes into her head of Pim in his burgundy-and-white striped rugby jersey passing the ball underhand, and on the heels of that the memory of Pim, in crisp khaki fatigues, carrying the Sword of Honour at the inter-schools parade. How can someone like that *know?*

She is aware that he is intelligent, but it is a Preston, McGrath and Bowyer kind of intelligence, not a searching-for-the-true-things intelligence. She is both terribly excited and horribly dismayed by this unexpected behaviour of Pim's. When she sees Pim again will she be able to tell? Will there be some signal? But how could she even allude to the search for true things without bruising herself? And especially to Pim, who laughs so carelessly, throwing back his head of golden curls.

Fat Betty wakes from a dream, sits up and catches sight of the whites of Lally's eyes in the dark.

'Lal-lee,' she says plaintively. There was always something oleaginous about Fat Betty, and these days it is worse. Since he was whipped for the firecrackers, Zulu won't speak to anybody, and Fat Betty feels his coldness most acutely.

'Shut up,' says Lally. She takes the instruction for herself as well. Since she discovered the ice chamber, she has been learning to give herself dry, clipped commands and to act on them absolutely, not hazing around in a welter of indecision like she used to. She pulls the duvet up to her chin and goes to sleep immediately.

Shopping

Lally is in Safeway, trying to choose a decent bottle of wine. Pim is particular about wines. Lally herself doesn't care much; she hardly drinks and, when she does, she drinks shots with the purpose of getting drunk. She selects a bottle of South African red on the basis of patriotic reinforcement and because it is slightly more expensive than its neighbours on the not-so-expensive shelf.

She is putting it into her shopping basket feeling a bit of a fraud, when she spots Ruth trawling her finger thoughtfully along a line of plastic bottles of soda and mineral water on the opposite side of the aisle. Ruth is looking for aerated water, but can only see plain. It's a wet, windy day for August and both the children are belted into stout green mackintoshes.

Ruth's elder son whines: 'You *said* we could have choc ices you *said* we could have choc ices you *said* we could have.' He turns around to kick at the wheel of the shopping trolley, in whose plastic well the toddler is standing up amongst cauliflowers and loaves of bread, and sees the exciting ostrich lady who came to dinner.

'I drew one!' howls Ruth's elder son.

Ruth looks up.

'I drew one,' repeats the boy.

'One what?' asks Lally.

'An ostrich, silly!'

'Oh.' How does one speak to children? 'Did it have a pink neck?'

'Huh?'

'They have pink necks.' Or do they? She seems to remember curving scarlet pipes, making heart shapes against the horizon as the birds canoodled.

'Mine was black,' says the boy, concerned.

'You shouldn't say silly to an adult,' says Ruth severely to her son. The toddler has started to wail in the trolley: 'I wanna draw a pitcher.'

'Hello, Laeticia,' says Ruth belatedly. She is conscious of her hair, which she should have washed. Her eyes stray involuntarily to the contents of Lally's shopping basket which are: a bottle of red wine, two pairs of stockings, a box of Cheezits.

Ruth's trolley, by comparison, looks like a relief package for a flooded third world nation – bread, fruit, vegetables, milk, frozen chickens, towering on three sides of her clamouring toddler.

'I'm shopping for my parents too,' explains Ruth. 'We're going down to Salisbury for the weekend. Mum's having back problems. She finds it difficult shopping and she can't travel any distance at all.'

'That's unfortunate.'

'We try and go down every other weekend.'

Lally knows about the back problems and every other weekend. The conversation is showing dangerous signs of grinding to a halt. Tinny background music from the store speakers is predominating. Ruth comes up with:

'I suppose you must feel rather cut off from your mother – being so far away.'

'I haven't seen her for several years.'

Ruth is shocked. Her own mother phones nightly to discuss the news and knitting dimensions for children's pullovers.

'We're getting choc ices,' says Ruth's elder son.

'*I wanna draw a pitcher.*'

'I had better go.' Ruth takes advantage of the toddler's

behaviour. 'He hates being confined. Why don't you come and have supper with us sometime?'

'That would be nice.'

No specific arrangements are reached, but it allows them both to part without awkwardness. There are a few more items on Ruth's shopping list, but nothing that can't be found in Salisbury. She trundles the trolley through the checkout counter, one child blustering about ice cream, the other about pictures.

Lally watches through the glass storefront window as Ruth signals to a cab with one hand and gathers her disarrayed hair against the wind with the other.

Half-term (Friday)

Aunt Caroline and Uncle Pim arrive at half-term to take the boys and Lally back to the farm. After breakfast, there is a brief chapel service. Because of the influx of mums and dads there is not enough room in the chapel for everyone, and lots of the dads elect to stand outside in the sunshine. The dads have beefy, heat-scored faces and wear safari suits and boots with knee length woollen socks in khaki and olive shades. While the service is going on, they smoke their pipes contentedly in the mild morning air, tapping down the tobacco when they refill the bowls and slapping old friends on the back (if they are standing) and on the knees (if they are sitting). Lots of the dads know each other from when they were in the boys' division themselves.

Inside the chapel, the mums wear light flowery cotton dresses and wide straw hats. All the mums bunched together creates an overwhelming volley of scents in the air – jasmine and petunia and honeysuckle. The pupils worm in the pews thinking of the four days of freedom that lie ahead. They sing various hymns with a liberatory theme, although not *Lord Dismiss Us*, because it is only half-term.

After chapel, the pupils hurry back to the dormitories to change into mufti and fetch their bags. In the girls' division everyone tells stories in high, breathless voices of what they expect to do over the half-term; of favourite ponies that will be ridden again, of far-flung sweethearts whose fidelity will be confirmed. All the chattering girls streaming out in their mufti makes the girls' division seem like a colossal budgerigar cage with the door left open.

It is hard to prise Uncle Pim away from his old mates, with whom he is swapping information about wool prices and notorious divorces. Michael, Ross and Lally squint anxiously into the sun while Uncle Pim chortles and exclaims, in his throaty thirty-fags-a-day voice.

'Darling,' says Aunt Caroline at last, tactfully, when she returns with Mark from packing his bag.

'Sorry, Jim,' apologises Uncle Pim humorously to his friend. 'Troops are on leave, hmm?'

Jim's own two *troepies* are shifting their feet and banging their bags against their knees just as fitfully.

The bakkie is parked a couple of streets away. Uncle Pim carries Lally's bag and Aunt Caroline carries Mark's. Aunt Caroline tries to hold Mark's hand, but he puts his hand behind his back and says: 'Aw, Mum, don't be soppy.'

Aunt Caroline, Uncle Pim and Mark climb into the front of the bakkie leaving the back free for Michael, Ross, Lally and the bags. It's the town bakkie, which means there is a canopy on the back and a fitted piece of mattress to sit on. The sound of Springbok Radio comes faintly through the glass partition between the back and the front. Mark is telling a story with hand gestures although Lally can't hear the words. Aunt Caroline interrupts the story with questions every now and then, and Uncle Pim rumples Mark's hair with the hand that isn't needed for the steering wheel.

They drive northwards out of town, passing the district where the Mackenzies live. Lally tells Michael about the television. Michael says that Uncle Pim is planning to get a set as soon as reception is extended to the rural areas.

'What about electricity?' says Ross argumentatively.

'It can run off the generator, same as everything else.'

'Televisions use a lot of electricity,' says Ross.

'They don't use any more than a light bulb.'

'Balls.' But Ross shuts up because he doesn't really know

how much electricity a television needs. He fingers his cic-atriced chin and stares moodily out of the window. Lally and Michael discuss science for a while – what will happen to the earth when the sun finally burns up and disappears, and whether that will be the end of God. Aunt Caroline raps on the window to tell Ross to leave his face alone, which is already stippled with old acne scars.

On either side of the northbound road hang farm signs with the name of the farmer and the farm and its specialisation.

P.V. VAN TONDER

MISVERSTAND

FINE DAIRY CATTLE

JAMES WORTHINGTON

WORTHINGTON'S REST

HORSE STUD

The fields are green with lucerne shoots, and squat red dwarf aloes and fierce orange *kanniedoods* grow on the cliffs that flank the roadside amongst the stubbly grass and na-ked brown rocks.

It is an hour and twenty minutes to the farm. The road twists over a series of low hills. At the base of one of these hills is a farm store, and standing on the road outside the store is a soldier wearing the Day-glo orange band of the 'Ride Safe/*Ry Veilig*' campaign. The Ride Safe campaign is to give our boys a helping hand. Uncle Pim slows the bak-kie to a halt, and the soldier runs to the driver's window.

'I'm only going about forty minutes along this road.'

The soldier asks if the *oom* will pass the T314. Uncle Pim frowns. Aunt Caroline says: 'You know, that's the dust road out to Meerspruit.'

'Oh … ja,' Uncle Pim agrees. 'Get in,' he says affably to the soldier.

The soldier climbs into the back of the bakkie. There are dark dun stains under his armpits and he smells strongly of stale sweat. His eyes have the blind, distended look of sleep deprivation. He murmurs hello and doesn't say anything else.

Michael asks him a few questions. It turns out that the soldier has just finished basics in a nearby training camp. Originally, he is from the Transvaal, and after he got his Standard Eight certificate, and before he was drafted, he worked as a mechanic for two years in Louis Trichardt. Ross is interested in engines and they talk desultorily about the subject for a while, but in the end the soldier is not very interesting. He is Afrikaans, and his English is not at all proficient. Whenever he says something the words come out in a hesitant, staccato stutter and his pale, dull, fatigued eyes strain goitrously against their lids.

Just then the Ride Safe ditty comes on to the radio:

Make a friend! Make an effort!
It's your duty and it's mine!
Make a point of picking someone up
At the Ride Safe sign!

'That's you,' says Michael.
'*'skuus?*' says the soldier, tiredly.
Michael gives up.

Uncle Pim speeds straight past the T314 and the soldier has to knock frantically against the glass partition. The T314 isn't much more than a track, winding off between fields of grazing sheep and patchy eroded grass. While the soldier heaves his army tog-bag and himself over the back ledge, Lally watches Aunt Caroline ask Uncle Pim if anyone will pick him up here, and Uncle Pim makes a response she can't decipher, but Mark's pouting little boy mouth shapes 'No, Daddy!'

Uncle Pim calls the soldier over: 'Will you be all right here?'

'Ja, *meneer*.'

Uncle Pim shrugs at Aunt Caroline and gives the soldier a warm Coke from the glove compartment. They leave him squatting patiently on his tog-bag on this subsidiary road off a subsidiary road, trying to get God knows where.

The tar road snakes on through the hills and on to a plain of level, yellowy grasses. At last they turn off onto the dust road that leads to the farm. They pass several signposts until they come to the sign which says Little Kimmeridge. The first Pim was from Dorset. Just inside the gates is the ruined cottage that the first Pim built in 1829, and that the Xhosas burned down in the frontier war of 1834. Subsequent Pims have kept the remains of the cottage as a kind of memorial.

In previous half-terms, Lally, Pim, Ross and Michael have played many rousing games of 'Kaffirs and Colonists' among the sombre, mildewed stones of the ruin. At first the farmworkers' children used to play too, taking the extra parts of warriors or foot soldiers in Her Majesty's regiments. But when Pim got to be the age Ross is now he was beginning to be the *baas*, and the workers' children were starting to be workers themselves, and they did not come to play anymore. Anyway, Pim did not want the workers to see him playing children's games. But they still played for a while without the workers' children. They took turns playing the different parts of Governor Somerset, King Hintsa, Chief Maqoma and Major-General Harry Smith. Chief Maqoma was the most popular role because, although he ends up dying on Robben Island, he also gets the most stirring lines. When Harry Smith sends for the chief and puts his boot on the chief's neck, Chief Maqoma gets to say:

'You are a common dog! This thing is not sent by Victoria!'

Beyond the cottage is a row of camps and lands and a horse paddock. Aunt Caroline is experimentally breeding Welsh ponies. There are already a pair of leggy spring colts in the paddock, and their overlarge, nervous heads jerk up at the sound of the bakkie. The last sweep of the road takes them past the lines of fruit trees in the orchard and the vegetable garden and they drive up to the farmhouse – a rambling, single-storey, tin-roofed building with a long, covered veranda and many windows, which has developed several strange annexes and accretions according to the whims of Pims.

A couple of collies chase the bakkie along the last hundred yards of road, which makes the confined bitches bark frenziedly in their kennels. Mark and Ross scramble out of the bakkie and tumble in the dust with the dogs. Mama Selena, the head maid, and her brother Cookie, the cook, appear on the veranda and smile, Mama Selena holding her hands in front of her broad, aproned girth. Most farm kitchens in South Africa have woman cooks, but Little Kimmeridge has Cookie. There are some exotic things about Little Kimmeridge because Aunt Caroline is originally from Kenya, and only came south after Mau-Mau. So, the cook is Cookie, and there is even a kitchen *toto* instead of a serving girl. The kitchen toto is Cookie's little son, September. Cookie goes back inside to his pots. The smell of stewing meat is already detectable on the air. Unusually, Lally feels hungry.

Another figure appears on the veranda behind Mama Selena and strides forward. It is Pim. He is much thinner than she remembers, and almost unnaturally fit. The corded veins are blue rivers irrigating his forearms and his chest is threatening to burst out of his T-shirt.

He shakes hands with Michael and Ross and hugs Mark.

He moves towards Lally and kisses her on the cheek. He smells of soap and the outdoors. She has not seen him for several months.

'How are things going, Lally?'

'Fine.' His voice is softer than it used to be, and deeper.

'Why dint ya come pick us up?' asks Mark accusingly.

'I didn't want to have to see Emily.'

There's an honesty about the remark which rather startles Lally. Aunt Caroline, who was fond of Emily, says: 'Oh, poppet, that's really not very nice.'

'I didn't want to have to see her,' repeats Pim, as if he didn't think he had been understood. His fair hair has been shaven very close to his head.

Before lunch, everyone gathers for beers and Cokes on the veranda. Pim and Uncle Pim smoke cigarettes. Pim has taken up smoking.

'You were so against it,' says Michael, who hates smoking.

'You get bored,' says Pim.

It is peculiar not to be able to talk to Pim about where he has been. Instead they talk to him about where he is going to go, which is to university. He has been accepted by the University of Cape Town to study business science. Uncle Pim does not believe that there is any necessity to take an agricultural degree – a farmer learns on the job – but there is a value to university, because men need to sow their oats in order to settle down. Uncle Pim met Aunt Caroline at university. As for business – well, farming and business are inseparable these days; it's not like the old days. You have to have your head screwed on, and you have to keep abreast of developments.

Mark thinks university is for tossers.

'I'm going to be a permanent career soldier,' he boasts. 'Like Major Carlton.'

He marches a soldier-march around the circle of easy

chairs. It is true – of all the boys, Mark is far and away the best equipped to be a soldier. Young as he is, he doesn't mind discomforts and he likes to live in a communal atmosphere aimed at a clear, invigorating purpose. When Uncle Pim and Aunt Caroline ask questions about school, Ross and Michael give short, dismissive answers, but Mark is full of enthusiasm. Nevertheless, he is incorrect in announcing that he will be a permanent career soldier. In fact, he is the only one of the boys who will never be a soldier at all. When he is finally old enough to leave the boys' division and follow his destiny, the black terrorist will have been released from jail, the wars will be over and the armed forces will be in the process of infiltration by the enemy. Fickle history! Disconsolate, Mark will be married early to the mild daughter of a farmer with no sons. But farming is no substitute for war, and Mark will grow increasingly frustrated, beating his wife, and then apologising and making love to her, and then beating her again, until eventually, despite her timid nature, she can't bear the cycle of bruises and sex anymore and files for divorce.

'Major Carlton is a schoolteacher,' Michael points out.

'Then why is he still "Major", huh?'

'Because he's a fuckin' lunatic,' says Pim unexpectedly.

There is a silence.

Aunt Caroline says: 'Shall we go inside?'

Cookie and September bring in the tureens. They are wearing the red fezzes and white gloves that Aunt Caroline managed to salvage when Jomo Kenyatta made off with her Kikuyu kitchen workers. They place the tureens on the warming trays, and walk back to the kitchen. The kitchen is at the far end of the farmhouse and Cookie and September's comings and goings are sonorously recorded by the yellowwood floorboards in the passageway.

The dining room gives directly on to the veranda on one

side and the west wall of the house on the other, with a view to the dog kennels and the more distant vegetable garden and orchards. It is a large, bright room, especially after midday when the sunbeams paint stripes across the white broderie anglaise tablecloth. On the walls are photographs of dead relatives from times gone by, standing with their feet on dead lions and elephants, and some more modern photographs of younger versions of Pim and Michael holding up braces of guinea fowl. Uncle Pim, Aunt Caroline, Lally and the boys join hands and Uncle Pim prays *for what we are about to receive.* Lally gets Pim's hand and Ross's hand. Pim's skin feels dry and there are callouses at the base of his fingers and on the side of his forefinger, and a tiny flickering pulse in his palm. Ross's hand is less interesting, and also less washed.

After lunch they take a nap. Lally is staying in the room she always stays in. The room faces on to the veranda but there are lace curtains over the window that prevent people going past from being able to see inside. She can see outside, and her view encompasses the yard where the bakkie pulled up this morning, the barn on the far side of the yard and a glimpse of the fields beyond and the kraal on a rise to the east of the farmhouse where the workers live. The room itself is painted in a dull pink colour and is full of girl things: a selection of old ivory hair brushes; bland-faced porcelain dolls arranged on wicker chairs; old, stained pictures of flaxen-haired girls on swings, and river boats. On the shelf are books for girls – the *Pollyanna* books and the *Anne of Green Gables* series and *Malory Towers*, which is about a British boarding school in a castle where nobody ever really gets in trouble and teachers called Mamzelle forget the curlers in their hair. There are joke collection books – Giles and Andy Capp and Dagwood. There are two iron beds with woollen patchwork counterpanes on them. The bedroom has a pleasant smell of dust and polish and old wood. When Emily used to visit, she had to share it with her, and Aunt Caroline would come in when they were both in bed and chat for a while in her nightgown with her hair loose over her shoulders. Then they would listen for the deep gurgling flush of the toilet in the main bedroom en suite which Aunt Caroline used before going to bed, and twenty minutes later a shape would materialise on the veranda and Emily would pad across the floor in her bare feet and climb out of the window.

'Only for kissing,' she told Lally sternly each time as she got her leg over the sill. When she came back, she woke Lally up briefly although not intentionally. In the mornings Emily yawned at breakfast and said: 'Heavens, Lally and I were chatterboxes last night.'

Lally lies down on the patchwork counterpane with a Giles book and feels happy about the fact that she won't ever have to share a room with Emily again. She must have fallen asleep, because she is suddenly aware of Pim's voice saying '… motorbikes.'

Pim is sitting on the bed. Her blouse has ridden up her stomach and her skirt has wound itself tightly around her legs. She sits up and wonders how long Pim has been there. He repeats: 'Do you want to ride the motorbikes?'

'Ja!'

She changes into jeans and boots and goes into the bathroom to splash water on her face. Outside in the yard, Uncle Pim has lined the bikes up and is testing the sound of the engines one by one and filling the petrol tanks from a watering can. There are only three 250cc bikes, but Pim is allowed to ride Uncle Pim's 500cc Suzuki. Uncle Pim hands one of the bikes over to her and she guns up the engine and circuits the yard slowly, changing up and down the gears and getting the feel of it again. Michael and Ross are already racing around the barn and the dog kennels, the nasal whining of the motorbikes pitching into a screech as Ross tries to change gear too quickly.

Pim appears on the veranda in jeans and an anorak. He walks over to the Suzuki and waits for her to complete her now less wobbly circuit. Aunt Caroline, Uncle Pim and Mark are in the cabin of the bakkie. Mark is protesting: 'Why can't I, Mum? I'm bigger than Broughton. I'm bigger than Fowlds.'

Broughton and Fowlds are boys in his class who are allowed to ride motorbikes. Aunt Caroline leans her arm placidly on the windowsill of the bakkie. Boys get motorbikes when they are nine years old, and there are no exceptions.

Uncle Pim steers the bakkie out of the yard and along the bumpy track that leads through the lucerne fields. Some of the fields are for maize, and he raises a small crop of pineapples every year, but most of the farm is wild land for angora goat browsing. As they clear the cultivated fields and come out into the wild land the boys drive their bikes off the track and into the veld, bouncing on the stones and slamming their legs against the ground for balance. Lally follows, feeling more confident now as her body remembers the bike skills.

'Don't spook the bloody goats!' yells Uncle Pim. The veld is teeming with goats in thick, end-of-winter coats watching the procession of bakkies and bikes with bleak, stupid eyes. He stops the bakkie and whistles to the three collies in the back, who leap out and start to circle the goat herd in a slouching run. Uncle Pim indicates a particular goat to the dogs and they corner it and quarry it back towards the bakkie, where Uncle Pim gets it in a kind of wrestling hold and peers inside its mouth. When he releases the goat it trots bleating back towards the other goats, its legs unsteady with fright and squeezed against the trunk of its body, like an incontinent old lady trying to reach the bathroom in time.

Ross tries to jump a ditch and comes off, grazing his arm on a fallen-down branch of a poplar tree. Uncle Pim confiscates the bike and loads it on to the back of the bakkie along with Ross. He drives on with Ross nursing his bloodied arm and trying to keep the dogs from licking at it.

The wind feels cold and fresh against Lally's face, and it is glorious to speed and bump over the imprinted tyre ruts on the track. They come out of the goat camp and go through a wire gate to a second camp which slopes down a hill to a reservoir at the bottom. Michael and Pim skim down the track and she tries to keep up. The reservoir is pearly in the late afternoon light, and there are traces of algae along the edges. Pim drops back and shouts: 'Let's swim after breakfast tomorrow, Lal.'

Uncle Pim halts the bakkie by the reservoir and takes an icebox of drinks from the cabin. He pours them all gin and tonics except for Mark, who gets a lemonade. Ross goes to the muddy edge of the reservoir and sinks on his haunches to sluice the blood off his arm.

Aunt Caroline has a happy, effusive expression on her face.

'It's been ages since we were all together,' she says. Her eyes are following Pim, who is drubbing his machine across trackless veld towards the far bank of the reservoir where a little thicket of poplars grows, all shimmying in the wind so that the light and dull faces of their leaves make a chiaroscuro pattern. Aunt Caroline is over forty, but at parties Uncle Pim tells his guests in a bawling good-natured slur that she hasn't aged an atom in twenty years. *Never guess she was the mother of four fine boys.* Aunt Caroline says affectionately, half-embarrassed: 'What a lot of nonsense!'

The light is fading. They drive back to the farmhouse and have supper, which is a simple affair of lamb chops and green salad and baked apple tart. Cookie and September left the chops and tart in the Aga and went up to the kraal at six o'clock. They eat in the kitchen and play Monopoly afterwards at the kitchen table. At nine o'clock everyone goes to bed.

Half-term (Saturday)

In the morning, the sun rouses her. It rises from behind the kraal, silhouetting the workers' compact, circular mud huts and grazing cattle against its great golden glare. The obscure clatter of morning activities has already started within the farmhouse itself.

Mama Selena and one of the housemaids are walking past her window with tin buckets in their hands. Lally says: 'Mama – wait!' She scrambles out of her nightgown and into her jeans and T-shirt and climbs barefoot out of the window. Mama Selena gives the housemaid's bucket to Lally and sends the housemaid back to the kitchen. The housemaid swings nonchalantly back along the veranda, her bare feet with flat pink soles slapping against the concrete. She is wearing an overall with a colourful cotton cloth tied around her bottom, and she is fifteen or sixteen years old and slightly pregnant. Mama Selena clicks her tongue. She is always complaining about the ineptitude and laziness of the under-servants.

When the chickens see Lally and Mama Selena opening the wire gate of the chicken runs they sit up on their nests and beat their wings agitatedly because they remember in their crazed chicken brains that human beings in their enclosure mean both gain and loss, but they don't remember why. Then they see the pails and remember about food. As

Lally and Mama Selena sprinkle the seed from the buckets, the chickens duck and peck viciously at each other, clawing in the dust with their grotesque feet. While their hard little beaks are stabbing at the ground, Lally and Mama Selena move from hut to hut, rifling through the nests for eggs to put in the pails. One or two sleepy or more maternal chickens have to be routed from their nests. They flap up on to their perches, squawking and boggling at the thieves with their tiny black unsettling eyes. Their cries are like scratches of sound.

Mark is capering around on the lawn at the back of the farmhouse in his pyjamas. Ross and Michael aren't giving up a late lie-in to do farm tasks, and Pim isn't given a choice, but Mark is still at an age where sleep is a chore. After carrying the buckets with their load of large, brown-spotted eggs back to the kitchen, Lally goes with Mark to look at the baby goats nestling next to their mothers in the hay. Pim and the men are feeding the calves in the calf enclosure. The calves butt their heads into the pails and come out with their soft sloppy muzzles doused in milk. Lally takes a pail and kneels in front of a newborn calf. She pushes milk-coated fingers into the calf's mouth and he sucks frantically, not moving his enormous guileless eyes from her face.

Breakfast is black Matabele porridge, eggs, bacon, sausages, toast, jam and tea. Michael and Ross appear sheepishly in their dressing gowns saying: 'Sorry, Dad.'

'Coupla pansies,' says Uncle Pim, who is eating a wad of bacon wrapped between two purposeful sheaths of toast.

She does go to swim after breakfast, but with Michael, not Pim. Pim seems not to be in a swimming mood this morning – he is quiet at breakfast, fiddling constantly with his napkin – and the skin under his eyes is shadowed. Anyway, Uncle Pim keeps diverting him with jobs. Michael and Lally take the two brood mares who are not in foal and canter along the track towards the reservoir. The morning is exquisite with the bewitching smells of saddle leather and grasses. At the reservoir, they wade through the mud until the water is up to their thighs and plunge in. They surface, gibbering with the shock of the night-chilled water.

Michael looks at Lally's body in her bright orange bathing suit and says: 'Lal, you really should try and eat more.' She shrugs, but when he turns to dive again she looks down at the bracket of her ribs underneath the nylon corset of the bathing suit. At breakfast, she ate half a slice of toast and fed the other half to the collie under the table. She feels a fierce surge of pride at her self-control. At lunch, Aunt Caroline gives her two potatoes and three slices of lamb, and she puts both the potatoes and one of the slices of lamb back. Aunt Caroline looks at her and Lally says defensively, 'My mother says I don't have to eat anything I don't want to.' Although Lally's mother, who eats like a bird herself, has never broached the austere silences of the carriage clock-dominated dining room so far as to make a reference to Lally's eating problems. Aunt Caroline looks argumentative, but leaves the subject alone. One of the advantages of not really belonging to anybody is that in the end you do escape many instances of specific scrutiny.

After the afternoon nap, Uncle Pim takes Pim and Michael out in the bakkie to look at the lands on one of his instructive drives. Lally has been along on several of these drives in the past. They usually consist of Uncle Pim explaining, Michael listening and Pim existing in a state of polite distraction. Uncle Pim treats Michael as a kind of helpful deputy in the cause of preparing Pim for his future. In any event, Uncle Pim's instructions won't necessarily be wasted on Michael – there are a good few farmers without sons in the district and a fair number of the daughters are setting their caps at Michael already (which development occasions Uncle Pim much ribald humour).

While they are out on the drive, Aunt Caroline and Lally sit in the easy chairs on the veranda; Lally reading and Aunt Caroline mending. Aunt Caroline looks reflectively at Lally over her needlework. She is fond of her old university friend, Lally's mother, and she is fond of Lally too and does not resent having her to stay over the half-terms. But she wishes the child was less remote. Having no daughter of her own, she would like to braid Lally's luxuriant ebony hair or teach her how to make pastries in the kitchen. But she can't imagine Lally encouraging such advances. She thinks, not for the first time, that the child would be quite pretty if she were not so scrawny and would smile more and would not let her hair hang in her face. Aunt Caroline thinks briefly of Emily, who reminded her more of herself at that age. A frolicking, chattering child with her fine gold hair and pale gold limbs. She used to sing all round the house like a little joyous canary. And yesterday she looked forlornly at Aunt Caroline during the service and all the light seemed to have gone out of her pretty face. Aunt Caroline feels almost angry with Pim about the loss of Emily. But you can't interfere with that sort of thing.

Mark is playing in the yard with September from the kitchen, and September's younger brother Goodwill. September is Mark's particular friend. Together they collect and blow out birds' eggs, float in tractor tyres on the reservoir, make clay oxen with the reservoir mud and torture or incorporate Goodwill, according to their mood. Mark, September and Goodwill jabber at each other in high, excitable voices that move erratically between Xhosa and English. They are playing a ball game originally designed by the fifth Pim – Uncle Pim's father. The ball game operates between two pieces of board – one nailed to the barn roof, and one to the chicken run fence. One person has to throw the ball at the barn board and sprint for the chicken-run fence. If the throw misses the barn board, the attempt at a run is aborted. But if it successfully hits the barn board, the catcher has to catch the ball one-handed on its downward descent and lob it at the chicken run board before the sprinter gets there. If he hits the board, the sprinter is out. The trick is that the irregular much-repaired nature of the barn roof makes an unpredictable business of both the ball's speed of return and its point of recovery.

Ross is lounging on the veranda steps, sulking. He would like to join in the game, but he knows his father would not approve and he doesn't know when he is due back. Ross is at an awkward age; too old to play with the *kwedins* but too young to go along on the instructive drives.

He claws at his chin. 'I'm going to bandage up your hand, Ross!' says Aunt Caroline threateningly. The throb of the bakkie is heard and then the bakkie itself appears, accelerating over the dust slough where the track merges into the yard and motored into the garage by Michael, who is driving. Uncle Pim is still explaining something about the eradication of poor grasses to Michael and Pim, except Pim has walked ahead of them towards the house. He half-kicks Ross, who crunches up his fists and feints a few punches. Pim pauses on the steps to watch the game. Uncle Pim and Michael push past him on to the veranda, and Mama Selena comes out with a tray of tea things.

At that moment, the farm worker Bheki comes around the corner of the barn, trundling a wheelbarrow of *phutu* and tripe mash that the maids have prepared on the wood stove behind the barn for the pregnant bitches. The mash has a sour unpleasant smell. Bheki is a stocky, muscular man of about twenty. He is wearing sleeveless overalls of the Farmer John type without a shirt underneath, and his bare chest is hairless and beaded with sweat. The overalls are a cast-off pair that used to belong to Pim. All the clothes from the farmhouse eventually have a second innings up at the kraal.

In the past, Bheki and Pim had much the same relationship that September and Mark now have. Perhaps this is what is in Pim's mind when he sprints down the veranda steps and wrenches the cricket ball from Mark's hands.

'Bheki,' calls Pim, and throws the ball hard against the square of board on the barn roof. He starts running a few paces, glances back over his shoulder at Bheki and slows up. Bheki is still gripping the wheelbarrow with both hands. He looks uncertainly at Pim while the cricket ball bangs against the board, jumps back into the air, meets the roof at a lower point and begins its zigzagging downward trajectory. Pim stops running altogether. The ball falls to the ground and rolls through the dust, stopping a few yards from Bheki. He picks it up with both his hands and holds it as if it were a grenade, his tongue working visibly against his cheek. Then he seems to make up his mind, and he throws it – not at the target on the chicken run fence, but back to Pim. He gathers up the wheelbarrow handles again and nods respectfully to Uncle Pim.

'*Baas*,' says Bheki, and wheels the barrow through the dust of the yard towards the bitch kennels.

The little tableau on the veranda has frozen. Only Mark remains kinetic, tugging at Pim's unyielding fingers to try and extricate the ball.

'Whatsa matter with you?' demands Mark, not realising that he is voicing the question which the rest of his family is trying to submerge. Aunt Caroline is the first one to snap out of it.

'Mark,' she says, 'tell the *kwedins* to go home. It's time for your bath.'

Aunt Caroline wishes she could so reassuringly order Pim to take a bath. Pim, who is turning the ball over and over in his broad hands; Pim who is frowning at the place where the tripe and *phutu* is being ladled into the dogs' dishes as if he had failed to understand something which should have been obvious. She turns to Uncle Pim, but he has gone inside the house without drinking his tea.

'Mum!' wails Mark, but Goodwill and September are already retreating, their small naked feet puffing the yard dust into a series of small dun clouds.

Procreation

'Ruth wants to have another child,' says Pim.

'Do you?'

'I don't know.' He runs his hand through his greying sandy hair. 'We can certainly afford it. And if she's going to do it, I'd rather she did it now than in a few years. I don't want an interminable continuation of having babies.'

Pim has been in the south of France for two weeks and his skin looks rosily suntanned against the whiteness of the sheets. There are three parallel grooves running around his neck which become more accentuated when he drops his chin. Lally traces her fingers around the grooves.

'Isn't it awful getting old?' asks Pim theatrically. He celebrated his fortieth birthday while he was in France.

'Oh, Pim, you're not old.' They have dropped Edgar and Laeticia, which was never all that convincing in the first place.

'Yes, but I'm not young, am I? When people speak about a young man they're implying under thirty, really, aren't they? Or early thirties at a stretch.'

'You're young-ish. Martin Amis is always described as a youngish writer, and he's older than you.'

'Yes, but he's got friends in the media.'

Lally laughs at that. Pim yawns and dozes for a while. He always falls asleep immediately after sex. Usually he says as he's going under, 'Make sure and wake me up in twenty minutes,' although today he doesn't have to. The falling asleep – which drives Ruth demented – doesn't bother Lally, who feels peaceful with his slumbering, contented body next to her. She watches him affectionately. He could, she reflects, take better care of himself. There is a sloppy rotundity about his stomach and thighs which he could get rid of with a bit of exercise. He has a very expensive gym contract, of which he never avails himself.

Pim murmurs and snuggles closer to her and stirs awake. He takes in his surroundings – the guestroom at home, and his present company. She sees a flash of concern cross his face, until he remembers that Ruth and the boys and the au pair are still in France for another week. His eyes half close and flicker open, and his lower lip slides reflectively over his upper lip.

'Lal?'

'Uh huh.'

'Didn't mean to sound negative.'

''Bout what, Pim?'

'About the baby thing. I love being a father. I'd potentially be up for another. It's just that the first couple of years are so disruptive and Ruth seems to get so consumed by it all.'

'Go back to sleep, Pim,' she says.

'Yes, I don't know why I … uh.' Another yawn upstages him. He recalls happily that he is not expected to chatter to Lally in this situation. She's an extraordinary girl, thinks Pim. Always has been … most … exs … ordinary … girl.

Saturday Evening

After supper, Uncle Pim and Pim have an encounter that is uncomfortably close to an argument. The disagreement arises just after they finish eating in the kitchen, and it is difficult afterwards to remember exactly what it was about, although the feeling of unease it creates persists. Uncle Pim had asked the boys during the meal if they would go on a *springhaasjag*, a chase after spring hares, with the aim of slaughtering them and reducing their numbers.

'Buggers are eating all my good veld,' says Uncle Pim.

After dessert, Uncle Pim takes the keys of the farm bakkie from his pocket and gives them to Pim.

'Stay on the tracks,' he tells Pim.

Mark is struggling into his anorak, which he has taken down from a hook on the back door.

'I'll fetch a *kwedin*,' he says indistinctly through the material.

'What for?' says Pim.

'For the gates!'

'You can do the gates, Mark.'

Mark's face emerges from the anorak, pink and indignant. A thorough *springhaasjag*, covering all fifteen camps of the farm, will involve a lot of gates and Mark's buggered if he's going to be responsible for opening and closing them. Fortunately, Uncle Pim says:

'Fetch September, Mark.'

There is a narrow, rather careful quality to Uncle Pim's voice. Pim stands up from the table. He says:

'I'll fetch September, Dad.'

'Mark will fetch September.'

Pim's fingers crawl restlessly down his cheek, dragging at one eye so that the bloodshot underlid is exposed.

'You can't send a seven-year-old boy up to the kraal with orders at this time of night, Dad.'

'And why's that?'

'Because it's not decent. They have their own lives.'

The kitchen is quiet.

Uncle Pim says: 'Whose workers are they, boy? Are they yours or mine?'

The relentless rumble of the generator seems unnaturally loud.

'Yours,' says Pim.

'Yours who?'

'Yours, Sir.'

Uncle Pim says, 'Fetch September, Mark.'

Pim says: 'If you fetch him, I'll whip your backside for you, Mark.'

Mark hesitates in the doorway, confused and insulted. There is a bright, watery film collecting in Aunt Caroline's eyes. Lally, with some astonishment, hears herself saying:

'I could get September, Uncle Pim.'

Uncle Pim turns his stony, reddening face towards her without moving his shoulders. It is suddenly remembered that one is in their midst who is not strictly a part of the family. He shoves back his chair and heads down the passageway towards his study.

Pim says, 'Yes, you go, Lally.'

She walks up the rise towards the kraal in the moonlight.

The kraal huts are arranged in a circle within a circular wire fence which marks the kraal off from the surrounding farm and contains the skinny cattle browsing within its perimeters. Between the huts are squares of cultivated earth on which maize and cabbage and other vegetables are grown. The highest feature in the kraal is the plastic water tank, which stands on top of three-metre-high iron supports with a pipe leading down from it. Uncle Pim and a team of workers lift the tank down from the supports once a week and take it down to the reservoir in the back of the bakkie to fill it up.

The front door of Cookie's hut, slightly lopsided in its mud shell, is painted a dull purple colour. Lally knocks and Mama Sizwe, Cookie's wife, opens it.

'*Molo*, Mama,' says Lally. 'The *kleinbaas* wants September.'

'September is not well.'

Mama Sizwe is not lying; Lally can see September lying on his bed of blankets inside the hut, rivulets of snot that weren't there this afternoon pouring from his nose. Mama Sizwe calls 'Goodwill!' and the smaller child appears from the shadows. As Lally sets off with him down the hill, his large eyes are apprehensive, but when he sees the bakkie and the array of wooden clubs and plastic-covered military torches in the back of it he becomes excited and makes a voluble series of remarks in Xhosa.

Mark sulks that Mama Sizwe has sent Goodwill instead of September. Apart from his personal preference for September, Goodwill is too small to manage some of the more difficult gates on his own, and it is clear in Pim's present mood that Mark will be expected to help.

Mark and Michael climb into the front of the bakkie, with Michael at the steering wheel, and Ross, Lally, Pim and Goodwill arrange themselves along the rims at the back. As they drive along the track towards the first camp, the headlights pick out two of the younger workers, Bheki and his friend Alfie, walking in their direction. Bheki and Alfie have been eating supper at the house of the overseer, who lives in a separate kraal on the northern boundary of the farm.

Pim leans over the side of the bakkie and asks the men if they want to come. He speaks in Xhosa and Lally doesn't catch everything he says, but Bheki peers into the front cabin to ascertain that Uncle Pim isn't in it and confers with Alfie. Alfie shrugs. The men hoist themselves over the tailboard and squat against it, talking softly between themselves. After a few minutes, Pim, who has been listening, cuts in with a comment that is obviously amusing because Alfie chortles and Bheki's dark eyes make a dry, sideways detour towards Pim. The awkwardness of the afternoon suddenly seems less real.

The bakkie bounces along the uneven track with the headlights and the torches playing over the veld as if the bakkie was a pin-cushion stuck full of pins made out of light. Michael and Pim smack their clubs gently against the palms of their hands. Lally is the first one to discover a hare. The beam of her torch, roaming across the grass cover, picks out the luminous twin discs of the creature's eyes inside its bunched little silhouette.

'There's one!'

'It's mine. It's mine!' yells Ross, springing out of the bakkie and battering across the veld in his sneakers. The sound of his voice and approaching footsteps breaks the hare's light-drugged trance, and it kicks off on its hind legs. But Ross has already got his club above his head, and brings it down hard on the crown of the hare's skull.

'Ace!' He picks up the dead hare by its feet and flings it into the back of the bakkie. The little body of the hare in the back of the bakkie brings on a bloodlust excitement, and they are all vigorously scanning into the darkness. Alfie and Bheki go after the next hare. Alfie's first cosh misses and the hare dodges away from him and towards Bheki, who manages to connect his club, but off-centre so that the hare is concussed but not dead, describing one frantic dazed circle before Bheki gets in with a second blow. The last blow makes the hare's eyes pop out of its skull, and the white bloodstained eye-sacs hang out of the hare's skull on to the floor of the bakkie. Lally successfully kills a hare and Pim dispatches at least a dozen in quick succession. Mark tries to kill several, but can't catch any. Eventually, Bheki and Alfie cheat by concussing one and shepherding it towards Mark, who heaves up his club and succeeds in breaking its spine rather than its skull.

Goodwill can't slide the wire noose of the gate to the fifth camp. Alfie starts to clamber out but Pim puts a restraining hand on Alfie's thigh and shouts:

'Mark, get the gate.'

Mark has been gloating over his efficacy in killing the hare, but now he is annoyed again and grumbles on the way to the gate and on the way back. He is at the centre of some game of Pim's that he doesn't understand. Lally can see him complaining to Michael in the front about the state of affairs. Michael shrugs and scratches at the hollow at the back of his neck.

The smells of earth and grass are strong in the cool night air. When they veer off the track, the crushed stalks make a spicy intrusion into the more general scents. A rain shower passed over the farm just before supper and the collected puddles give off the flavours of water and mud. A hare is running ahead of the bakkie, dodging this way and that way in the glare of the headlights but not breaking into the grass cover where it would stand more of a chance. It is surprisingly fast, and Michael accelerates and gives chase. In the back of the bakkie the passengers perched on the rims sit on their hands to keep their bottoms from slamming painfully into the metal. Michael is gaining on the hare. He looks critically at the little sprinting brown body, steers the bakkie fractionally to the left and steps on the pedal. A plume of blood sprays outward from the inside front wheel.

Bheki climbs out. He picks up the flat, eviscerated object and, grinning, holds it up for inspection.

'Charming,' says Michael. 'Chuck it in – the dogs can have it.'

Bheki adds the hare to the growing mound of bloody dun-and-white fur. They've been going for a couple of hours and there are about thirty hares in the pile. Bheki, Alfie and Goodwill start to divide the hare-heap up between themselves. They will take the hares up to the kraal to be skinned and cooked. A game develops with the scrambled hare, which is too damaged and dirt-caked to be considered a spoil, but Bheki and Alfie keep finding ways of getting it into Goodwill's pile when his attention is diverted. After a particularly stiff gate, Goodwill returns and rifles suspiciously through his pile, finding the hare about two-thirds of the way down.

'Fok you all,' he says, extricating the hare and thumping it on to the summit of Bheki's heap. Goodwill is a spirited if very small child.

Lally is laughing. She turns to Pim to see if he is laughing too, and notices that he is not laughing. Pim is huddled in a rather odd constricted posture in one corner of the bakkie. He left off the hare-killing a while beforehand, and she had assumed he was bored with it or out of breath. She switches her torch on and directs the beam at his face. He has gone a peculiar whitish-green colour and his bloodless lips are working against each other. His eyes are fixed on the abundant hare blood that is sluicing up and down the corrugated indentations on the bottom of the bakkie.

'Pim?' says Lally cautiously.

His head bucks back when she says his name. He stares at her, startled, as if she was someone unexpected.

'Pim?' Lally says again.

But he has already vaulted out of the bakkie on his long legs and is striding away from them across the veld. Lally taps on the cabin window, Michael brakes and his head pokes enquiringly out of the side window. She points to Pim's disappearing, already indistinct form. Michael frowns and scrapes at his front tooth with his forefinger.

'Don't ask me,' says Mark from the other front seat, holding out his hands in a palms-upward gesture.

'No one was going to,' says Michael shortly.

It seems upon reflection that it is already quite late – Mama Sizwe will be fretting for Goodwill, and Lally and the boys have to be up before eight to go to the rotating Sunday service on another farm. They jolt back over the maze of tracks and drop the workers at the kraal, helping to ferry the armloads of hares to the huts and kicking at the excited African dogs who release strings of drool when the smell of blood and meat brings them out of their night-stupors.

At the farmhouse, there is no light coming from Pim's window, but they don't know whether he is asleep or not back yet. Uncle Pim has already gone to bed and turned off the generator. They make coffee in the kitchen, using the gas stove, and take turns in the bathroom to brush their teeth and shower off the blood and sweat.

Alone in the bedroom decorated for the daughter Aunt Caroline does not have, Lally is restless. She fiddles with the lace trimmings on her nightgown and brushes out her hair with the ivory hairbrush until it puffs around her face like a cloud of coal dust. She pulls the wicker armchair up to the window and sits for some minutes with her feet propped up on the sill. Then she gets up from the chair and goes over to the three-quarter mirror that is part of the dressing table. She looks at the shape of her body underneath the nightgown and bites her thumb knuckle. She takes a pot of cream from the dressing table and rubs the lotion into her hands.

Up at the kraal, the dogs begin to bark and the breeding bitches in the wire enclosures behind the house wake up and yip-yip in reply. Before the barking dies down, Lally, without thinking much about what she is doing, has blown out her candle and returned to the wicker armchair.

Pim enters the yard. She thinks he will come into the house through the kitchen door, but instead he turns and walks in the opposite direction towards the barn. The entrance to the barn is on its west face, looking towards the orchards, the pony paddocks and the vegetable garden. The barn doors are two enormous squares of tin. She watches Pim tug one of the squares ajar and disappear through the gap. The square is shifted back again from the inside, although the door does not close entirely.

Perhaps Pim has disturbed an owl in the rafters of the barn, because a low mournful hooting breaks the tyranny of the night stillness. Her window makes a resistant creak as she pushes it up and her feet *push-push, push-push* over the rain-damped dust of the yard.

The barn is as black as lake water, except for the open place where the walls don't quite meet the roof and the stars are visible. Also, there is a diffuse mist of light ahead of her which seems to have no source. At first, she can't understand, and then she realises he must have lit a lantern and gone behind the bank of hay bales which Uncle Pim keeps in the barn to feed the horses and the dairy cattle. The light is pouring through the chinks between the bales.

When she reaches the edge of the stack of bales she expects to see him, but is instead confronted with what appears to be only another ordered yellow face of hay. She takes another few steps forward and comes upon a kind of roofless hay-cave where a dozen or so bales have been removed from the stack. Pim is sitting in the middle of the cave on top of a pile of karosses made from impala skins. The lantern is in a shallow tin bucket to prevent it from falling over and setting the hay on fire, and there are a number of books scattered around the edges of the kaross pile and a couple of folded-up Basotho blankets.

He is resting his head on his drawn-up knees and when she appears in front of him his eyes are already on her, so she supposes he must have heard her approaching footsteps.

'Hey, Pim,' she says.

'Hello, Lally.'

His eyes settle on the lantern. She looks at his face to determine if he would rather she wasn't there, but he seems, in a preoccupied way, to be glad that she has come or at least not to mind, so she climbs on to the low bank of bales and sits down next to him.

'Where did you go?'

'Swimming.'

She can see that his hair is still damp. Pim is fiddling with a piece of hay, making an incision in the top of the shaft with his fingernail and then splitting it along the fault line. She finds her own piece of hay and plays with it.

'How is Emily?' he says after a while.

'Disappointed.'

He looks up at her.

'She was so excited,' expands Lally, 'about … you know.' She touches the lieutenant's star place on her own shoulder.

'Ah,' says Pim. He looks back at the light. After that she is quiet for a while. Eventually she says:

'I like it in here. Do you remember we used to play here when it was raining? In the haystacks. Afterwards, in the bath, the water burnt the places where the hay broke my skin.'

'Yes,' he says.

'Are you going to sleep here?'

'Yes,' he says. 'Sometimes when I seem not to be able to sleep in the house, I come here.'

'I don't sleep well a lot of the time.'

'I used to go out like a light,' he says, 'Now I just lie in the dark and think.'

A mouse scuttles across the barn floor; an insignificant brown flash which makes a prolonged shrill squeaking as it disappears into a crack between bales.

'It's all right, Pim,' she says.

'No, it's not all right.' He turns his head, which is still resting on his knees, towards her and she sees that his eyes are bloodshot and shadowed again as they were this morning. 'I would like to think it was all right, and I've tried to pretend it's all right, but it is so far from all right that it's just not a possibility anymore.'

He shakes his head as if he is shaking unwanted detritus out of it. 'The stupid thing is not that I stopped being able to believe in it, Lally. The *stupid* thing is that we can't possibly win. It's going to go on and on and on in the most nameless and impersonal and unspeakable way, without the faintest chance of us ever winning. A few million mad burghers against the whole of Africa and the whole world and the whole tide of history. And if we stopped now – Lally, that's the thing. If we only stopped now and tried to think and plan ahead we could still …'

He breaks off and pulls at the corners of his mouth with his hands.

'That's not even worth thinking about because it's never going to happen. Do you know something very strange about the *situation*, Lally? Up in Angola – I expected to find the situation there, and when I got there I found it. I certainly found it. And then later it came to me that Angola was only where the situation *seemed* to be. The real situation – it's right here. It's in every city, every village, every township, every farm … we're right in the thick of it. It's in our faces. It's in Mark's face. He's a seven-year-old boy, and he's got a war in his face that he doesn't even know exists.'

'We know it exists,' she says. 'We see the army.'

'But you think it's a defending army against a threat from outside. We're the threat, Lally. Our obstinacy is the threat. And we can't see that we're threatening ourselves too.'

She nods. She has guessed as much. But he is looking at her tiredly.

'I don't expect you to understand. You're just a child. I suppose you have some boyfriend at school who takes you to dances and carries your books for you.'

'I'm not a child. I don't have any boyfriend.'

'Why don't you?'

'I'm not popular.'

'Why is that?'

'I'm not … fun.'

'Yes,' says Pim reflectively. 'Fun is terribly crucial. I was tons of fun. Do you remember? I was a laugh a minute. It's when the fun stops and you have to think about the other things that the problems start. But you don't know.'

'I do know.'

'No, you don't. I didn't. What do you think your days are about, Lally? Do you think it's about sport and lessons? That isn't it at all, Lally. The chief purpose of every single day in your life is to teach you what to hate and what to adore. And to programme you to be terrified if you forget which is which and to be scornful and angry if other people look as if they have forgotten. That's what school is, Lally – it's a training ground for citizens. In a couple of years, they're going to send you away hating and adoring exactly as they wanted you to. You don't know, Lally.'

'I do know,' she says. 'I don't know enough, but I do know a bit.' And she tells him at last about the doubt and the chamber of ice and the search for true things. At first the right words are hard to find, but as she is stumbling in the midden of words a kind of compassion comes into his exhausted, concentrated face and all her thoughts pour out in a flood.

'Oh, hell,' he says when she is finished. 'It's no good. We're full of poison.' He places his hands flat against the tan-and-white markings of the uppermost kaross. He looks at them.

'Me worse than you, Lally. I went away kicking my heels, hating and adoring, ready to be a man.'

He holds up his hands in front of him.

'Look at them, Lally. They are the hands of a murderer.'

He puts his head back on to his knees and sobs. She watches him uncertainly. She doesn't know what to say. She might hate and cry out in fear against the war that has no name and no geography, but she will never be called upon to be one of its warriors.

'Oh, Pim, please don't cry …' she whispers, but she is crying herself. She puts her hand against his cheek, where it looks small and pale, although the light from the lantern gives her skin an aureate cast. Pim's rough, wet cheek strains against her hand as the calves strain against the milk buckets. After a few minutes, he looks up at her and sniffs twice, noisily, wiping his nose on the back of his sleeve.

'I'm so sorry,' he says softly, 'you should just go to bed.'

'I don't want to.'

'I'll be all right.'

He reaches out and touches her shoulder reassuringly. She moves her cheek against his hand. Pim was going to say something more elaborate, but instead he says:

'Ah.' His fingers have found the lace trimmings on her collar and are working against the material.

'Ah,' says Pim again, inarticulately. She nestles closer to

him on the kaross and he buries his nose in her hair.

'I didn't think,' he is murmuring. 'I didn't think I … you …'

You have to be humble about language. And sometimes the only language which can prevail is the language of bodies. The only thing she was always able to control was her own body. As she kisses him, she unlaces his boots, unbuttons and removes his shirt and jeans, his socks, underpants and wristwatch. She pulls her nightgown over her head.

'Oh, my Lord above,' says Pim. Emily sometimes allowed him to touch various parts of her body in this very same barn, but the path of persuasion was so elaborate and enervating and the event itself so vigilantly stage-managed that he felt more like a weapons inspector than a lover. But now he feels like a lover and, pushing up on his hands, he is relieved and encouraged to see that she is smiling beneath him. She is suddenly very pretty when she smiles, which he tells her.

'Am I doing this right?'

'Oh, Pim … how would I know?' she says, which is both a disarming and an alarming remark.

He jerks out of her gasping and his semen splashes across her thigh. He lies against her on the kaross, his arm thrown across her stomach, and the shape of the lantern blurs into a haze. She watches him fall asleep. The slick on her leg has a distinct, unusual smell, glistening and winking in the lantern light. She tastes it on her forefinger. Is it more like nuts or more like earth? Or is it outside comparison?

She feels happier than she can ever remember feeling before. The terrible crime of sex is, in fact, the most sublime, the most touching, the most human act conceivable, although she has watched a thousand farm animals do it a thousand times. And how unexpected that Pim, of all people, who carried the Sword of Honour at the inter-schools parade, who appeared in school plays hammed up as a nurse, should turn out to be one of the ones who knew.

Because sex, which was meant to be so bad, was so good, she is tempted to believe that there is an exact inverse relationship between what the authorities say and what the truth is. But she knows that is too easy. The construct *what they deny is true* holds all the inherent faults of the construct *what they say is true*. She must still get at the truth in slow and self-revealing nuggets, fed through the ever-widening filter of her own discernment.

'Lal,' mutters Pim, stirring. 'You better wake me up ... in a while ... 'fore Dad ...very early ...'

'OK, Pim,' says Lally.

Part Two

A Second Letter

At the top of the page on the left-hand side is the green, black and gold logo of the Commission with its curious ovals and crescent waves. Opposite the address of the Investigative Unit in Cape Town and beneath the logo, her own address:

Upper Addison Gardens
Kensington w14
London

So proper and English-sounding, but giving a false impression because the road is at the furthest extremity of Kensington, really more Shepherd's Bush, and the house itself, on its bustling corner, any objective bystander would declare as being on the Holland Road thoroughfare.

Underneath the address is her name, and then:

Re: Human Rights Violation Investigation: Sipho Qhashane

The Truth Commission Human Rights Violation Committee will be holding a public hearing on November 18th at the Community Centre, New Brighton Township, Port Elizabeth. Mrs Nomda Qhashane will be giving evidence about the disappearance of her son, Sipho Qhashane. We understand from her that you might have some useful information relating to his disappearance to assist the investigation and corroboration of her story. We would be very grateful if you would send us a statement of all the information that you might have.

Yours faithfully
Theuns van der Merwe
Investigator

Who are these shadow-people who follow her and send missives from a far country? This unknown Theuns van der Merwe; this Mrs Nomda Qhashane, who is known; this Sipho Qhashane, who is known? How can you respond to such a correspondence? But equally, how can you throw everything in the bin? She folds the letter and slots it back into its envelope. She turns the envelope over several times in her hands and puts it away in her pocket.

The Concupiscence Of Pim

Pim isn't impotent, but he needs quite a bit of initial encouragement. Sometimes, after a long day of mothering and home maintenance, Ruth will find Pim limp but hopeful. Who can blame Ruth if she thinks 'let sleeping dogs lie'.

For Lally, it is different. Pim's penis is not the stuff of marriage, the staff of custom, but the flagged pennant of the past. Lally is holding history in her hands. Also, Pim's condition is a double-edged sword; a cloud with a silver lining. If Pim is slow to wake, he is also slow to die.

Right now, the arisen Pim is underneath Lally. He feels himself hardening and the first tremor of imminent ejaculation, and the little mental *ouch* that intermittently accompanies ejaculation and makes him suspect that his infant circumcision left him too tight. But when he finally asked the doctor to have a look, the doctor suggested a minor operation and Pim's buggered if some tosser with a knife is going anywhere near his prick.

Because it is Lally, Pim allows himself to be flooded by a wave of sexual patriotism. In his mind's eye, the girls of his adolescence sprint athletically across the baked crusts of sports fields – sun-burned Amazons with lean muscular shanks, pertly shuddering breasts harnessed beneath burgundy tunics, fountaining blonde ponytails gleaming in the sunlight.

Foolhardy Pim! If the memory of the girls of his youth excites him, it also makes him anxious. The past is a cornucopia of vivid emotions – some transporting, some disquieting, some demoralising, and some to be avoided. Pim's penis, torn between utopia and unease, exactly imitates the penis of his elder son at this very moment, hidden inside his bathing togs as he waits at the side of the school pool for the swimming master's finger to descend on him. He comes and goes – a beat of life, a thoughtful whelk, aimed at future action.

Lally's eyes open and she gazes down at him between sheets of hair. She is curiously ageless, he thinks, even now, almost twenty years from the first time they made love. Remembering, his nostrils catch at the ripe scent of hay, the paraffin odour of a lantern, the furry blunt emanation of a kaross. He is, after all, having what amounts to an affair. Spurred by this thought, Pim strides on to glory.

Afterwards, he falls asleep. Lally feels rather restless. Ruth and her entourage are coming back from France tomorrow, and Lally is not altogether sorry about it. It feels good to be with Pim, sexually and amicably, but they have seen each other every day this week and it is making her edgy. She doesn't want to get enmeshed in complications. She likes Pim; likes him strongly, both the collected Pim of the present and that other inevitably lost, though more stirring, Pim of the past. But she has never been in love with him. She's never been in love with anybody.

'I can't accommodate to love,' she has tried to explain more than once to men who, enraged, have found themselves alone in the condition.

Pim has fallen asleep in a sprawling way that has left her trapped in a wrap of sheets. She looks out at the room from her sheet prison. He always insists on the guestroom; he doesn't want to be unfaithful in the bed he shares with Ruth. The guestroom is pleasant but anodyne – a room designed for nobody in particular – Laura Ashley curtains, a double bed, a white-painted bureau with a basket of potpourri on top. It is a Zulu basket, the geometric designs woven in darker strands of reed. The house is full of unobtrusive African things, she's noticed – carved walking sticks, beadwork, footstools – only they obtrude because they don't look right, nestling amongst the rugs and against the radiators. A zoo for artefacts. She works her arms against the confining sheet until it gives a little, and wriggles out. She pulls on her panties and bra and dress and goes into the bathroom to try and clean up. While she's swabbing with a clutch of tissues she thinks, *I could dislodge the diaphragm and see if I get pregnant.* But it is not really a serious thought; more of a kind of game of deviancy – like imagining standing up at a wedding when the minister asks if anyone knows of a reason why this man and woman should not be joined in matrimony.

The bathroom window shows a powdery-blue square of evening light, a nearby rosy cloud bisected by the neighbour's chimney, a more distant skid of purple against the horizon of roofs. There is a framed photograph on the sill of Pim and Ruth on their wedding day. Ruth looks incredibly young – not much more than an adolescent, her light brown hair with its vague curls garlanded in white flowers and cascading on either side of her comely, not-quite-plump face. 'What was I doing at that age?' Lally thinks, and for a moment she can't remember and is assailed by a cringe of self-pity. She feels annoyed with herself for allowing an emotion that will only lead in upon itself.

This upstairs bathroom is the children's bathroom. On the tiled banks at the end of the bath are untidy pyramids of rubber alphabets and clockwork ducks and helicopters. These articles feel incongruent with her being here, and she feels another invasive tremor of – well, anyway, not guilt. She objects to feeling guilty about anything because she's paid already, paid in advance, for whatever future sins she might commit. Paid in blight. Blight, she says at her face in the mirror above the basin, a blighted life. And cries a bit, standing up with her cheek against the wall, snivelling on cold tiles with Thomas the Tank Engine motifs stickered to them. Although, when she goes back in to Pim, she will be neutral and careless. Will not inflict.

The phone rings three times and stops. Pim's strident modulations are sleepy at first, and then more alert.

'Give him Nurofen then if the Calpol has worn off,' Pim is saying. There is a pause. 'Oh Ruth, come on, man ...' (he still says *man* like a South African when he is exasperated) '... don't be alarmist. He always does that. No, everything's finished from the freezer. I'll order something. I honestly wouldn't bother taking him in, unless you give him the dose and his temperature doesn't come down. It's a big hassle and they'll send you home and tell you the same thing.' Lally edges into the bedroom and Pim puts his fingers against his lips warningly. 'OK, put him on.' Another pause and his voice becomes more jocular and curiously soft. 'Hello, scamp. Are you being a bugger?'

Lally goes out of the room again – a refugee from intimacy – and loiters on the landing. Through the flimsy material of her dress pocket she can feel the rectangular, certain shape of the letter against her thigh.

1979

Standard Nine
Geography and Destination

Lally is in Standard Nine. As far as she had thought about it over the Christmas holidays, it seemed Standard Nine would be much the same as Standard Eight or Standard Seven, except that all her classmates have generally gotten taller and even those with late-budding breasts have come home from the holidays with new bras in crisp cardboard boxes. But, from the moment of arrival, it is quite clear that Standard Eight was a holiday by the sea in comparison to what Standard Nine will be.

In October, the outgoing prefects will be relieved of their duties so that they can concentrate on the national examination, and the new prefects will be selected from Lally's year. And even in February and March no one is forgetting that for a second. Children who let their hems come unstitched or ran in the corridors last year are suddenly on model behaviour – everyone's uniform is spotless, no one is ever late for anything. But that's not enough. There is no use in being without fault when everyone is without fault. So, the children begin to find ways of catching each other out and reporting the misdemeanours. It has to be sly, because who wants to look like a sneak? The best way is to talk about the felony within earshot of the teacher or the matron while pretending you haven't noticed their presence. *Where's Ellen? Didn't she know she was on litter duty?*

I expect she's been given a detention again. Didn't she have detention last week? What's happened to Ellen? She used to be so organised and take such a lot of pride in being a member of the school, but I can't help noticing more and more ...

Even Lally, who does not want to be a prefect, who cannot imagine writing sternly in an order booklet or turning on a swift admonishing light in a chattering dormitory, is affected by it. All the children watch each other with narrow calculating eyes. Conversations are riddled with chary scepticisms. They confide in each other about who might be rising and falling in the polls and traduce their confidants within the same day. Cartels form, disband and reform. But the least secure ones, the cherry-biters without qualities, are perhaps the most malicious, and only get more so as it becomes apparent that headway is not being made, and desperation mounts. So those who were nearest to being her friends are now the least trustworthy. She does not blame them.

The life of a prefect compared to the life of an ordinary schoolchild is one of boundless freedom. The prefects can go out for a chocolate milkshake at the cafe on the high street any afternoon they choose, and see movies on Saturdays, unaccompanied by the staff. Their rooms in the annexe are spacious and comfortable and they can sit on the prefects' lawn with its benches and fountain and green, watered shrubs and chat to the boy prefects for as long as they like and the teachers don't mind a bit. And beyond all that, they cannot be punished. When the final selection is made in October, a massive fealty re-establishes itself amongst the *chosen*. Even if a prefect infringes a rule, the others will turn a blind eye. And the opposite is true. They watch the skulkers like the Government watches those known to be in sympathy with the banned terrorists. Without being a prefect, the final year will be a dreary, endless, humiliating trap. During these crucial months, even the most humane and least self-interested of the children cannot afford to let opportunities slip. So, she cannot blame them, but talks to no one.

Related to all this is the great anxiety that arises in Standard Nine over the question of cubicles. The girls' division building has three floors and an attic. The ascent of students through the hierarchy is geographic as well as ideational. On the ground floor is the girls' dining room, the matron and the under-matrons' rooms and the dormitories for the smallest children. The bulk of the girls live on the second floor. The third floor is reserved for the Standard Eights, Nines and Tens, and the prefects in the annexe.

But the question of geography and ideation is at its most acute and pressing on the third floor. Or perhaps it could be seen as a question of geography and destination. Because things are not as simple as they might seem for the Standard Nines on the third floor. On the third floor, a bed is not merely a flat spongy surface to lie down on; a locker is more than a metal case in which to store one's belongings. The beds and lockers have all become part of a complex system of politicking and apprehensive sycophancy.

The east face of the third floor is the Standard Eight dormitory, from whose vantage point Lally liked in the previous year to watch the cadets. The west face contains the bedrooms for skulkers – not as large as those for prefects, and partitioned with plyboard instead of brick, but still fully enclosed spaces with independent lamps rather than strip-lighting on the ceiling, and with closing doors.

The Standard Nines don't have dormitories or bedrooms. They sleep in cubicles – three-sided partitions of plyboard curtained off at the fourth end. The Standard Nine accommodations are between the Standard Eight dormitory and the skulker bedrooms, opposite the stairway to the prefect annexe, the main stairway and the ablutions – a line of rectangles of fluttering cotton and chipped edges of plyboard. At least this is where three-quarters of the Standard Nine accommodations are. There is not quite enough space along the corridor for all the cubicles, so a few are situated off a smaller corridor at right-angles to the main corridor, on the west face, just past the skulker bedrooms.

On the face of it, the cubicles near the skulkers have all the advantages. They face west rather than north, and the prevailing northerly wind that always plagues the valley in the hot months does not affect them, whereas for the main corridor cubicles there's a choice between stifling to death in the summer from a closed window or having your business on periodic display thanks to a rogue breeze-blown curtain. Then there is their comparative distance from stair noises, bathroom noises and prefects.

But it is this last putative asset that is really the crux of the thing. It is a known fact that the proximity of the skulker bedrooms to the west is a contaminating influence and that the outgoing prefects, who bring a weighty *jus divinum* to bear in these matters, do not bother to patronise those who live remotely. There has never in the history of the girls' division been a prefect picked from among those allocated a west-facing cubicle in the selection term, and even those who found themselves there in the first and second terms are courting disaster.

So, as the children pile out of the buses and cars on the first day back from the Christmas holiday, there is none of the usual bantering and loitering with old pals for the Standard Nines. Instead, the Standard Nines leave their bags unattended and head hastily for the postings on the dining room wall. Those in the undesired rooms sulk and chew their lips and drag their bags upstairs thoughtfully. With skill and persistence, there will still be time to effect a change by the second term, but it's a tricky thing and an unmistakable setback.

Lally sees that she is posted along the skulker corridor in what is in fact the most lowly cubicle of all, because it is the last in the row at the furthest extremity from the promising cubicles. Fat Betty is next door. Fat Betty is so desperate to upgrade that she battles her shyness and goes to speak to the matron, the head of the girls' division and eventually the headmaster himself. But to no avail. When they come in from the buses at the start of the second term she's been shifted two cubicles towards salvation, but she's still on the west face and her fate is as good as sealed.

Lally does not ask to change and is left where she is for the whole year. She is not unhappy with the room especially. It's in the corner of the building, which means it's a little cramped, but also bricked on two sides, making it almost like a real bedroom. In the summer, the bricks remain cool to the touch. She's the last port of call during the morning inspection, leaving her with nothing more to deal with than a whipped-aside curtain and a hurried nod. And the view is pleasant. The girls' division building is only five hundred yards away from the boundary fence. On the far side of the fence is a pineapple farm, and there is a big pineapple field directly opposite her window. In January, the field of dry summer-yellowed grass is stippled with rows of vigorous green pineapple plants. In the centre of each plant is a small ripening blue-green fruit. By March, the pineapples are big and yellow and ripe. After the picking and the passage of winter, the broad-based tapering leaves turn slowly from green to yellow. She likes to wake up early in the morning and watch all the permutations of colour, and the workers in their blue overalls hoeing or picking or operating the big tanker of the spray boom pulled by the tractor along the grassy swathes between the rows.

On the near side of the fence in the lot between the girls' division building and the boundary is what is known as The Plots. Some of the boys who cannot pass mathematics are given the option at the end of Standard Seven to take a subject called 'agriculture' instead. There is a practical component to agriculture, which focuses on the cultivating of pumpkins and beans and maize in The Plots. The agriculture boys – beefy, squinting, thick-necked, of closely-related parentage – come from the most outlying and unproductive farms in the Eastern Cape and are largely an under-motivated crowd. She never sees them at work, as they labour during the hours given over to maths, but The Plots have a mournful neglected air of unpruned vines and smothering weeds, and every now and then there are fights and a pumpkin smashed in the dirt to tell the tale. During the long break at Christmas, the school gardeners get The Plots to look after, which seems to agree with The Plots, because they always look healthier after the holiday.

On the northern edge of The Plots stand the compost heap and the new shed and the old shed. The new shed is a sturdy vibracrete structure with a galvanised zinc roof, where the barrows and tools are kept for the gardeners and the agriculture students. It was a present from the matric leavers in Pim's year. Before that, the school had to rely on the old shed – a small and sorry affair of untreated tin with a wooden meranti door. No one's bothered to patch up the old shed since its retirement, and it is very dilapidated indeed. Everyone agrees ought to be demolished but has not yet been on account of The Plots not being a part of the school frequented by visitors. In the meantime, the rotting door has been boarded over with pine and the boards nailed down to prevent naughty children from sneaking cigarettes in there, but the roof is cankered with rust-holes and even the pine boards are starting to moulder.

There are other things that are different this year apart from the worry about the prefect elections and the cubicles. Now that they are in Standard Nine and almost grown-ups, they have a special citizens' class. It is called 'national preparedness', and they learn things in national preparedness that they need to know in order to be responsible South Africans. National preparedness is Major Carlton's brainchild. In other schools, they have 'youth preparedness', which is about saying no to cigarettes and touching your privates, but in this school they have national preparedness, which is far more serious. National preparedness is one evening a week in the auditorium. The auditorium is unlike any other room in the school. Major Carlton has raised all the money for it himself with a cadet display and other lateral-thinking ideas. Everything is state-of-the-art – an overhead projector and a cine projector and a slide machine, and the chairs slope down on an incline so that you don't have to try to see over anyone's head.

Although Major Carlton is the teacher for national preparedness, because it is not really school he calls himself a 'discussion leader'. To illustrate the point. he wears a cardboard badge on the chest of his regimentals that says *Discussion Leader.* They all have to stand up at the first meeting and promise to God that they won't scare the little ones with what they learn in Nat Prep. That's what they call it after a while; Nat Prep. But Major Carlton's concerns are unnecessary, and not because of the vow either. In the beginning, the lectures are a diversion. They hear about how, if the blacks were ever to overpower the whites, the country would be called Azania ('Azalea like the flower, Sir?' calls McGrath, and for once his quip is discouraged, because Azania is too serious). In Azania, all the population would live on socialist farms called *kolkhozes* and schools like this school would close and reopen as communist Azania schools, and the children would wear a different uniform with a pillbox hat and a high-throat collar instead of the burgundy tunics, shirts and shorts they wear now. Major Carlton has some slides of children wearing the communist clothes in Russia and Cuba and China. A lot of people in Azania would die before Azania got very old anyway – from revolution if they are white, and from poverty and tuberculosis if they are black.

But pretty soon, despite the innovations of the discussion leader and the state-of-the-art equipment, everyone is bored to tears with Nat Prep. It's just all the same, with charts and dates and photographs of short, stubby guns called AK-47 Kalashnikovs. So, no one listens, and no one remembers enough to tell the little ones. The only good thing is when Major Carlton shows slides and short films, because he makes the room dark and the children who have sweethearts can hold hands in a way they would never dare in the classroom.

In August, Bowyer brings great credit to the school by winning the Sword of Honour. The Sword of Honour is awarded annually to the best cadets in the country. The best cadets are given a chance to shine at the annual displays. On the day of the annual display for the Eastern Cape, all the white schools from far and wide converge on Port Elizabeth. There is a military marquee for the displays and a brass band and a buffet in an enormous tent with every conceivable delicacy and oxen on spits turning behind the tent. The school sends two kombi vanloads to the annual display – one kombi with Bowyer and the senior cadets, and the other with the prefects who are girls or who aren't in the senior corps (there is one boy with great potential who only has a leg above the knee from falling under a tractor as a toddler). The prefects are sent to be spectators and to give support.

It is a heady day – apart from Bowyer winning the Sword of Honour, the senior corps gets a medal for precision marching and a special mention for uniform and appearance. At the prize-giving, Bowyer gets to mount the VIP platform and shake Prime Minister PW Botha's hand and the hands of half-a-dozen brigadiers and generals and to kiss Tannie Elise on the cheek. Afterwards, he carries the sword in the victory march around the marquee. Bowyer holds the sword in the salute position; the hilt at his nose, the blade pointing up, unwavering and stern at the head of the senior corps in the burgundy rugby socks and epaulettes to show which school they are from. Everyone is as proud as punch, because it's been a long story of disappointment and failure and seeing the sword go to other schools since Pim won it and carried it in the victory march four years ago. It is an absolute certainty that Bowyer will be head boy now. But you can't give all the credit to Bowyer. As the headmaster points out at assembly, although Major Carlton, with only two years of service, is a relative newcomer to the staff, his dedication and vision have raised a flagging corps to become one of the best, if not the best, in the country, notwithstanding the Afrikaner schools who cheat by giving over actual lesson time to training.

The sword is displayed in a glass case in the entrance hallway of the school block. But that is not the end of the glory. The police brigadier for the district was so impressed by the conduct of Bowyer and the senior corps in general that he has contacted Major Carlton to ask if he can give an address, and Major Carlton has invited him to talk at Nat Prep. It is not at all a usual or expected thing, because the brigadier is an elusive and reserved man and, what is more, is known to have turned down numerous invitations to speak at the Afrikaner school in the town of Suurfontein in the next valley.

On the occasion of the brigadier's address, they all have to go to Nat Prep fifteen minutes earlier than usual so that they will be seated and quiet by the time he arrives. Everyone is grumbling because of missing seconds at supper. They expect the brigadier to be a powerfully-built man because of being such an important policeman, so when he comes through the entrance of the auditorium and Major Carlton motions for the scholars to stand up, it is a little vague at first whether this really is the brigadier, despite the blue uniform and the decorations, because he is so slight and slender for a full-grown man. He's not all that much bigger than Zulu, and he is markedly smaller than Preston, McGrath and Bowyer.

But by the time the brigadier has crossed the room and they have all been looking at him for a couple of minutes, he seems to have grown. It's not that he isn't still small. It's something other than that. He seems to have expanded, as if he owns the air all around him, and it's taken on substance and become part of him. Lally finds it disconcerting. She bites on the metal part at the end of her pencil, which holds the tube of rubber, and waits.

The major introduces the brigadier. He makes some remarks about his achievements and the strength of the district police under his guidance. The brigadier seems unaffected by this flattery. He stands very still and erect. His eyes are a curious shade of flecked gold, as if they were two miniature apricots, picked at just the right moment, sitting in his head. The eyes seem very focused, although it is hard to tell exactly whom he is watching. It appears as if he is looking at everybody, like the portrait of the Mona Lisa. He has a trim pencil moustache of the sort that the Afrikaans people call a *snorretjie*. Every now and then, he smoothes the *snorretjie* by drawing the back of his middle finger carefully along its length, like a cat preening.

The brigadier steps forward to deliver his address. He has a soft way of speaking; almost mellifluous – the words come quickly but crisply from his mouth. The title of the lecture is 'Black Violence'. Except it is actually '*Swart Geweld*', because he speaks in Afrikaans. Which is a mistake, because a lot of the scholars can't follow him. Perhaps the brigadier does not realise that this is the most exclusively English school in the district. Afrikaans is not popular or particularly encouraged, beyond the national requirement to pass it for university entrance. It isn't even offered as a first language. But, in the event, the brigadier only talks for about ten minutes, about when the blacks started killing and history stuff like that, which they already know from other Nat Prep lessons, and shows a few slides of bomb victims. The fact of his talking for only ten minutes is a relief because of the Afrikaans, but also problematic because of leaving forty-five minutes of Nat Prep to fill up. It's easy to tell that Major Carlton is a little put out, both at the Afrikaans (which is a language he doesn't understand at all) and at the brevity of the address. The brigadier offers to answer questions, but no one puts up their hands because of being shy to ask the questions in Afrikaans and maybe make a mistake with the grammar. There is something about him that makes you more anxious about making a mistake than usual.

Major Carlton goes to his classroom to fetch some slides with which to enlarge on the topic of *Swart Geweld*. When he returns he is slightly breathy, and there is a dent in his brow which makes it apparent that he has reached the conclusion during his exodus that the brigadier is simply not playing cricket. He makes a bit of a song and dance while he is slotting the slides into the projector, stressing that they are about to see footage of a 'Real War Situation'. Some people start giggling because there is plainly a bit of one-upmanship going on between the major and the brigadier. The major wants to make it crystal-clear that he has come from a 'real war', whereas South Africa is not really having a real war, just the trouble with the blacks. The brigadier doesn't take offence. He calmly watches Major Carlton's technical preparations and touches his moustache.

The major goes off at a tangent about the Second World War as well, and the brigadier remarks that his father was in the *Ossewa Brandwag*. That nearly finishes the major because the *Ossewa Brandwag* were Nazis, and Nazis are bad because they killed, with no conscience, Jews, who, in the final analysis, are just white people from foreign parts and with a different culture. Moreover, Nazis bollocked the King. The major's acrimony towards the royal family is reserved strictly for the present Queen, and he feels a warm regret and sympathy towards the memory of the dead King about the disgraceful behaviour of his daughter in the matter of foreign affairs and Empire.

There is a rippling undertow of giggles at this point about the brigadier being the major's special guest, and the major not liking him because his people were Nazis and he's a rockspider Afrikaner. The major starts to ignore the brigadier. He announces that the slides show what the disloyal Shona did to the loyal Shona in the Rhodesian Real War situation. He flips a switch at the back of the slide projector and the giggles stop abruptly. Some of the girls scream. The pictures are horrible. It's not just missing limbs like the brigadier's slides, but missing skin too and tips and ears and the most terrible burns and people strung up on posts with let-me-die expressions on their faces. The major keeps flipping the switch and intoning the names of the places where these atrocities took place in a sombre voice, like some sort of dirge.

Lally starts to feel a panic coming on. Sweat is collecting

on her palms and at the back of her knees. The metal taste is in her mouth. Lancets of chemical poison are spiking her heart and the air is thinning fast. She closes her eyes and holds her body rigid – still, still, still – forcing her consciousness away from the slides and the major and the brigadier and into the ice chamber. *What is, is not. What is not, is. Other than it seems. Always something else.* The major's death-dirging slide soundtrack – *Chipinga, Umtali, Elim Mission, Vumba* – grows dimmer and static and indistinct, borne away on seeping ice-floes. The frost-rent drifts of the ice chamber press mercifully against her eyelids and temples, driving away the panic. Seracs and bergs; frozen, unmoving. Motionless torrents, silent cataracts. Herself snow-hung, numbed, escaped within the inescapable.

When she thaws, she is moored in the alert gold eyes of the brigadier, but then so is everyone else. The children are getting into their blazers, boys hotly saying how they would deal with any political kaffir that came onto their farm and did anything like that to one of their workers. The sirens for junior lights out are sounding from both the boys' division and the girls' division, which is the signal for the end of national preparedness. Lally puts on her blazer as well and joins the queue shuffling out of the auditorium. As she reaches the door, she glances back at the brigadier. He is chatting casually to Major Carlton as the children file out; his small, balanced body close to the major's squarer, tardier one, and fixed in an attitude of listening to the major, shoulders turned attentively towards him. Major Carlton has recovered since showing the slides and evidently feels that he is back in the driving seat. He expands about some matter – Lally can't hear what – and the brigadier pays polite attention. Leaving aside the cultural faux pas of the Afrikaans and the *Ossewa Brandwag*, the brigadier has not been one shade less than courteous to Major Carlton since he appeared through the door. But Lally is developing a sense for real intentions, and what she sees withheld in his gold eyes is amusement.

A sudden understanding comes to her. This Afrikaans man did not come to their school to tell them about *Swart Geweld* or to congratulate Bowyer. He came to be amused; for a diversion on a rural Wednesday night. With funny, pompous Major Carlton from Rhodesia and all the English children with their serious cadet corps and their serious Nat Prep that he observed in passing at the annual display. He made a fifty-minute drive over the hills and plains to their town for the purpose of mocking Major Carlton. He has been mocking Major Carlton with his incomprehensible speech and his apparently innocuous mention of the *Brandwag*, like Preston, McGrath and Bowyer mock Zulu. Except that this brigadier is different from Preston, McGrath and Bowyer in that he is so self-contained that he does not even need the children to know he is mocking their teacher. He is just having fun with himself. And, for some reason, this scares her terribly.

Nomda

Without her really understanding when or how it happened, he became a man. There is a different feel to a home when it has a man in it – when a man lives there – and one afternoon it came to her. A man lives here now. And on the heels of that thought, another thought. *He* is the man. My son. Which brought pride, but also sadness. And worry.

She is confused by this precocious manhood of his because he is still too young to go to the bush, yet he wants to behave as if he had come from the bush already. She does not have the money to send him to the bush at this time anyway, nor a close male relative to make the arrangements. And where will she make space in the shack for a man when he gets back? In the meantime, he is getting out of control. Because it is different with the schoolchildren now, she thinks, since the time of the riots in Johannesburg, Even in this small place. And while she is still pondering how to send him to the bush, trouble comes.

He stopped playing soccer. He was becoming so skilled with soccer – along with the hard balls of muscle in his upper arms and his calves and the increased height came a grace and a powered precision, the bare calloused surface of his foot kicking the ball to the places that his eyes sought out. And he runs fast. Every afternoon, the first few days after he stopped, the red and blue boys from the Fingo Pirates came and called from outside … *Hey, Sipho, come and play.* But he didn't want to any longer.

He has started with questions. The questions are disrespectful and judging of her. In the white man's shop in the high street he asks: 'Why do you call him *baas?* He's not your *baas.* You don't work for him.'

'Shhh! *Hayi thula!*' She hisses at him in consternation, wheeling around to see if the white man has heard. 'You don't work for that man,' says the boy again, stubbornly. She's always irritable with him. He sits under her feet in the shack with his angry face and his accusing queries. 'Where's your homework?' she demands in retaliation. 'Where are your books?'

'It's just Bantu Education.'

They have a fight about it. He throws the Bantu Education books on the floor and stamps on the splayed spines. She is appalled. Even the girls are scared. They do not tease him any more. Then he stops going to school altogether. He seems dissatisfied with everything, loafing around the shack, listlessly picking at patches of oxidisation on the walls.

He starts to go out again. He goes at night. He does not say where he is going, but sometimes comes back when she is getting up for work and the sky is already grey. He can't avoid her because he sleeps on a mattress on the floor of the main room with the big double bed in the corner that she shares with her mother. She says: 'Where have you been? Where, Sipho – where do you go?' But he only grunts and lies down on the mattress, pulling the blanket over his head and ignoring her. There is no evidence of alcohol or dagga on his breath. At first, she thinks he is going with a woman, and she is disgusted that he would take a woman before he has been to the bush. But she sees from his reserve with the girls his sisters bring to the shack that he is still without experience. And he does not smell of women either, in the dawns. But his voice, which no longer stammers between high and low, is hoarse as if he has been talking through the night.

She is never relaxed about the boy any more. Because

there is one she is afraid of. They are all afraid of this one
– all the mothers and the fathers. Only the schoolchildren
are not afraid – and that is because they are still children,
these newly-grown men and women who stamp on books,
and they don't know enough to be afraid.

The one that they are afraid of, they call The Leopard.
Die Luiperd. She has seen him on three or four occasions,
always in the passenger seat of a yellow van which a junior
policeman drives around the township. Looking and looking. She tries to think that they could just be looking for
drunks. When she was a girl, the police drove like that
through the streets – just looking for drunks, and no one
was very scared of them, even though it was stricter in that
time with the curfew for blacks. The first time she came to
visit in the town from the farm she forgot to pay attention
to the curfew time, and when the siren went she had to run
hard through the streets and the people were leaning out of
the doors and laughing.

But it is not like that any more. Nowadays, they don't
laugh. And the doors are shut. The third time she saw Die
Luiperd it was just outside her house. He called her over
and said to her in her own language:

'*Molo*, Mama – what have you been doing?'

'Shopping, *baas*,' she said. She was still holding the
shopping bag.

He looked at the bag and touched his moustache with
the back of his long finger in the odd way he has, which is
one of the reasons they can him Die Luiperd.

'And is this Mama's house?'

'Yes, *baas*.'

He nods politely. But she knows that with policemen it
is better if they shout and give orders. At least you know
where you are. Her eyes slide over to the young white policeman in the driver's seat. He is staring straight ahead,

141

and the thick blueish neck veins running under his red skin are prominent with tension. She can tell he is also nervous of Die Luiperd but has to sit all day in the van with him, just inches away, while Die Luiperd interviews this one and that one. She feels a little sorry for the young policeman, but also cross with herself for having the sorriness.

One night, the boy comes in just after midnight, rousing her from an uneasy slumber. She does not have the energy to have it out with him yet again, so she lies in bed, pretending not to have woken, relieved at least that he is home. She will just let him get on to his mattress and leave it alone. But he comes over to the bed and shakes her arm.

'Mama!'

She stirs a little.

'Mama. I'm in trouble, Mama.'

She turns to him wearily – weary for the trouble he causes, weary for everything.

'Just stay here,' she says. 'Don't go out like this all the time.'

'Mama!' His voice is high, stricken, whining like a child's. She wakes fully and sits up in the bed, causing her own mother to twitch away from her. She sees that he is sweating, his dark eyes distended and blinking rapidly, breath sucked gaspingly into clenched lungs. The arm of his jersey has a ragged tear, as if he snagged it on something while running. Fright vibrates through her so violently that the fright is physical pain.

'It's too late, Mama. Here is the most dangerous place.'

Her heart jumps once, hard, hurting. But she is his mother again.

She goes to get her headscarf and coat from the wall pegs in the other room, which is the room for storage and for the daughters. The daughters are wide awake now, clutching each other and their blankets and staring at her with big, startled eyes. She motions to them to stay where they are and returns to the main room.

'I know where,' she says.

Voting and Politics

'I wouldn't *not* vote for the ANC at future opportunities because of that,' says Pim, 'but it just leaves a bad taste in the mouth.'

'What does?'

'The not-voting. The no postal votes. As I was saying, that consideration alone wouldn't change my vote. But I do find it odd. And I feel excluded from the process.'

'Find what odd?'

'Lally!' he says exasperatedly, as he might say to one of his boys. 'Concentrate!'

'I don't know what you're talking about, Pim.'

'Not having been able to vote in June. Because of being here. Because the ANC wouldn't allow postal votes. Didn't it bother you?'

'I didn't realise that was the situation,' she explains. 'I don't vote.'

Pim looks as if he's swallowed a fly.

'What do you mean you don't vote? How can you not vote?'

'I did once. I voted Labour once.'

'But how can you not vote for … us? Here, it's just mind politics. There, it's blood and soul politics.'

She shrugs. 'What's the difference? You wanted to vote and you couldn't. You don't even live in that country anymore.'

'But I wanted to vote, Lally! I even thought of flying out to do it. If it hadn't been the middle of winter there, I would have done it.'

'I'm sure the leaky-shack-dwellers cursed the winter for

keeping you away.' He leaves it alone for a while. Then he says argumentatively: 'What about '94?'

'What about it?'

'You must have voted in '94. The first democratic election? You must have wanted to be a part of that?'

'I didn't,' she says, parodying his tones. 'Want to be a part of that.' She makes a mock-appalled face.

'Well – I don't understand you. I did fly home to vote in '94, and there *was* the option of a postal vote then. I wanted to cast my vote in the land where I was born. I wanted to be there.'

'Oh, Pim!' She has to laugh at this swashbuckling. 'You big patriot. You went home that time to show Aunt Caroline the new baby.'

Pim feels annoyed and casts through his mind for a scathing put-down with which to parry hers. Sometimes he gets in a mood to be sexist. Ruth is uncomplicated in that way. Any woman admitting to the moniker 'feminist' makes her look anxiously for the nearest exit, thumbing her wedding band for reassurance. A guest once left a copy of *The Female Eunuch*, and he found Ruth clutching the book and squawking in horror, having read the bit about needing to taste one's own menstrual blood. Soothing in some ways, her compliance about the precedence of male needs can be vexing when one is trying to provoke.

'That's very womanly, isn't it,' is what he comes up with now as a Lally-dig. 'Aren't you being a bit of a bird? Not making the effort to participate in the public forum?'

That should infuriate her, being a girl who travels alone, is promiscuous, not bothered with kids and all that. But she only says:

'Perhaps.'

Pim looks around Lally's room, considering the non-impact of his skewed barb forlornly. The room does not offer much stimulus in the way of ammunition. They are both lying on a futon he bought her recently because he was tired of her single bed, which was very cramped with two people in it and creaked alarmingly when he got down to business. It isn't even so much a bed as a nasty iron cot of the hospital throw-out variety that the landlords of places like this seize on so gleefully. Pim is not, at the age of forty and pulling in the sort of disposable income that he is, prepared to make love on a creaking single bed, like a student. However, when he presented the futon to her, having hauled it from the back of the taxi and staggered up the three flights of stairs to her room with it, she regarded it with an air of doubtful aggression as if it were some kind of malign force intruding into her home, and made no move to relieve him of his burden.

'What am I going to do with it?'

'Sleep on it, of course,' said Pim, offended at the indelicacy.

'But what about when I go?'

'Where are you going? You haven't said anything about going anywhere.'

She adopted her inscrutable-mask expression, leaving Pim with an unappreciated-gift feeling. It was a very respectable futon too – he could have got a used one through the classifieds – but he had had the taxi driver stop on Kensington High Street while he ran into British Home Stores. He only managed to budge the unappreciated-gift feeling the following day by buying the boys remote-controlled trucks with Pokémon designs from Harrods' toy department and allowing himself a gratified soak in their unrestrained howls of delight.

She still sleeps on the iron cot when she is alone, and the futon stays rolled up against one wall, awaiting his visits. This gives it a raunchy association in Pim's mind, at odds with its white-linened eastern aesthetic.

Pim sighs. He holds his hands out in front of him and flexes them, staring intently at the shape of the square palms and the ten strong digits stemming from the palms as he does so. It is a habit he developed as a young man. He does it when he is worried or perplexed or frustrated, or even just wistful. But the gesture carries its own cell-memory emotions. It soothes him to look at his hands, but it also makes him sad in a tired way.

'I did go to show Mum the baby,' he admits at last. 'That was the ostensible reason we agreed to go – Ruth and I. But I really did want to be a part of the voting. To be there when I did that. I really did want to feel part of things.'

'Well, I didn't,' says Lally.

Inanition

She has a friend.

The friend does not know that he is her friend. She has had him for only three or four days, but he fills her mind. In the classrooms, at inspection, in chapel, in the dining room – she is carrying the knowledge of her friend like a talisman against evil. He is a secret friend – hers alone. She is utterly sure none of the other students or the teachers know about him. But he is not imaginary.

At the beginning of the term, she does not have him. At the beginning of the term things are very bad. It is the third term of the year – the selection term for the Standard Nines. A fortnight after the school reconvenes from the spring holidays, the teachers and outgoing prefects enter into a series of pow-wows. During the pow-wows, the whole of Standard Nine collectively holds its breath. The week of the pow-wows crawls by with agonising tedium. It is as if they are all caught up in a slow-motion film. Or sealed in a jar of vinegary aspic, squeezing their eyes shut against the acidity, trying to budge their limbs against the thick, congealing jelly. The prefects come back at night from the meetings, smug and secretive, their pow-wow files in their book bags held close against their bodies, giving nothing away. For once, there is a horde of other insomniacs besides Lally. She can hear them pacing and flushing in the ablutions when she's up at night. They are all pumping with adrenalin at the rumours – rumours about who is being discounted, who is being favoured, and more grand-scale rumours about the consequences of not being a prefect in the afterlife. Someone is certain that Rhodes University does not accept non-prefects; another that the University of Cape Town will accept a skulker, but will not offer residence accommodation, which scares them all because they are rural children and hardly any of them have relatives in the cities. The rumours fly through the cubicles in the night like motes in a dust-storm of fear. In the daytime, they sit in the classes, wan and exhausted, their eyes bagged and shadowed, unable to hear anything the teachers are saying.

At the Monday assembly at the start of the fourth week, the announcements are finally made. There is an outbreak of kissing and squealing amongst the girls, and the boys manfully shake hands. Standard Nine is neatly divided along lines of horror and relieved ecstasy. Lally sits glumly. She is now officially a skulker. Beside her, Fat Betty gasps. Tears leaking from her eyes, she knots and re-knots her hanky on her lap, forcing herself eventually to get up from her chair, fix her face hurriedly with her blazer sleeve and congratulate Major Carlton's daughter, who has become head girl. Major Carlton's daughter nods austerely, aware of her position and responsibilities and the unbreachable social gulf that now yawns between her and Fat Betty.

After the selections, Lally stops eating. Never having had much of an appetite, she cannot surmount the nausea that rip-tides through her body in response to what is happening all around her. She moves the food around her plate, forking up the occasional mouthful and grinding it laboriously to a super-processed pulp before swallowing, her eyes trained on the map of the world. After a while, this behaviour is noticed. Because she is in the same year as the prefects now and there is the danger of rebellion, she is moved to the top table with the head prefects and the teachers for supervision. The head prefects and the teachers force her to eat. Every meal is a crass burgundy blur of admonitions and fingers pointing at her plate. There is a rule that you have to eat what you take, but now the food is spooned onto her plate for her and she has to eat it, even though she did not help herself. Apart from the nausea, she resents this bullying terribly and finds it intensely humiliating. So, she starts to vomit after the meals, although she is not a classic bulimic: she has no desire to binge – every mouthful she ever puts in her mouth feels foul, alien, infected. It is as if what she is being forced to eat are nuggets of the prefects and the teachers themselves. To make herself vomit, she pictures the authorities rotting on a gibbet – the diseased flesh coming away in lumps on to her plate. After the vomiting, her stomach feels disburdened, but there is a sharp bile taste in her mouth and her teeth feel thin and grainy.

Most distressing of all in the third term is the onset of a sudden inability to access the ice-chamber. It is as if all the hot ambition that surrounds her has melted the ice-chamber and she is stuck in a scorching world of cinders to be branded and burned. When she tries to go to the still, cold, isolated place, where she has managed to retreat intermittently for over a year, she just can't reach it.

The loss of her refuge is an unmanning blow that makes her nerves jar against the confines of her skull every time she fumbles for the secret world and finds the pathway vanished. Added to this is the nausea, the insomnia and the heavy legacy of the coming year-and-a-bit that must be lived through as a skulker.

But living is a choice. No one can force you to live; not if you are determined. There are always unguarded moments, an unforeseen method by which someone who is tired of living can ebb away from the flames. Dying – who can know anything about dying? – and there is still enough of the fear of the Christian mythologies in her to make it an intimidating thought. But the fear of dying is a different and more remote thing than the frantic and sapping exhaustion of living.

Suicide – the option of suicide – is her new resource. She thinks about it constantly – hatching little plots, subtle strategies. The nurses at the sanatorium work in eight-hour shifts and she begins to frequent the san at the start of each shift, complaining of a pressing headache and begging a couple of aspirin from a fresh nurse. A fortnight after the selections, she has accumulated a stash of fifty-seven aspirin in an empty film canister. But it does not seem possible that fifty-seven aspirin will be sufficient to halt the life processes of a healthy sixteen-year-old girl. Particularly one whose stomach is accustomed to regular regurgitation.

Her mind turns to jumping. The third floor is quite high. The window of her cubicle is large enough to admit her narrow body, but it is heavily barred. However, when she examines the bars she sees they are riveted to the window frames with screws that do not look especially forbidding. She crouches by the window in the long, warming late October nights, noiselessly coaxing out the screws with her penknife. It is slow but steady work and, by the end of another week, she has three out and five to go. The drawback is that this finicky labour gives her plenty of time to think, and what she thinks about increasingly towards the end of the week is the matric prefect with potential and a leg above the knee, who fell under a tractor as a toddler. People sometimes survive accidents or non-accidents. She pictures herself at the top table, paralysed, in a wheelchair and with a neck support, the prefects and teachers shovelling her full of liver and onions and sago pudding, and herself unable to throw up afterwards.

The rest of the Standard Nine year has settled, joyfully or gloomily, into being prefects and skulkers. While Lally has been sitting in class turning such concepts as *pills/rope/swimming-pool-in-a-heavy-coat* over in her mind, a new craze has arisen. There are often crazes during the October/November cusp. The matrics are on Swot Week – the week's leave between classes and taking the national examination – and most of them have left for their farms or the farms of friends. This gives the Standard Nines a taste of what next year will be like, and makes for a kind of giddy spiritedness among the prefects. The new craze is just for boys, but also tremendous fun for girls. The craze is streaking. Streaking means running around outside in your birthday suit. Boy prefects can get away with this sort of thing because it's good clean fun, and because of boys-will-be-boys. There has already been one streak around the school block and the sports fields, but it was in the very early hours of the morning and no one saw the boys doing it. Now the boys are planning a much more daring streak, which actually entails leaving the school grounds. Many of the girls are giggly and silly about the streak and are planning to catch the boys at it, and take a peek at their you-know-whats.

The streak-whispers gust and rustle around Lally in a *frou-frou* of hushed feminine voices. One maths lesson, sitting digging at the pitted desk with her compass, she thinks she will somehow orchestrate her jump with the streak, land on Preston's head and break his neck. Dead, butt-naked Preston with an astonished limp you-know-what and dead nightgowned Lally, the opportunistic murderess/seductress/suicide all scrambled up at the foot of the girls' division. This thought makes a sudden sharp ejaculation blast up from her unsteady stomach and into her mouth – a sound halfway between a laughter-hiccup and a sob.

The maths teacher looks up, surprised.

'Laeticia?'

'Sorry, Sir.' She can feel hot tears coming on fast. 'I need the bathroom.'

He gives her permission. The male teachers are always lenient with the bathroom, because of periods. She clips along the corridor at a quick trot and gets into the lavatory cubicle in time for a soundless flood of wailing and a quick retch for good measure, although her stomach is empty already.

Shortly after this incident, during another wide-awake night, she is fiddling with the screws again (although she has basically discounted the jumping hypothesis) when she is alerted, at a subconscious level, to the fact that something unusual has just happened at the edge of her vision. She puts the penknife down on the window ledge and frowns, poking her head through the bars and leaning forward into the night air to inspect The Plots. She is sure she saw something briefly that did not seem to fit, but she is not sure what it was that she saw.

Then she sees it again. It is the wooden meranti door of the old shed. Or rather, the rotting pine boards on the meranti door. They are shifting. She is sure of it. It is easy enough to discern the movement in the moonlight because the meranti wood is dull-reddish and the once-varnished pine boards are a still patchily refulgent yellow-white. When the boards shift, she can make out that they are covering a sizeable rot-hole in the door. And as she is peering uncertainly, a head – a black man's head – appears through the hole, scouts to the left and the right, and withdraws.

It's not possible. But even as she is thinking this, the head reappears. This time it is face-up and followed by shoulders and a body as the figure wriggles on its back through the hole and stands up, dusting soil from its trousers. It's not really a man, more of … a boy. A Xhosa boy. There is a log a few yards from the old shed, and the boy goes there and crouches down and feels beneath it and finds something there. She can't see what it is, but from the way he holds the object in his hand, tearing at it with his teeth, she realises it must be food – probably bread. Still tearing and chewing, he returns to the shed and slides back on his bottom through the hole. His hand re-emerges to wipe away the slide-marks, the boards are hefted back into place, and he's gone.

It is the most anomalous thing. Why is there a boy – a black boy – there? *There?* What is he doing there? How did he get there? Whose boy is he? There can only be one explanation. There is trouble. He is in trouble. He is hiding.

All thoughts of suicide are driven out of her head. All she can think about is the boy. There is a person – another person – awake in the night, and he is scared. She knows he is scared – she knows fear, and although she could not make out his expression clearly in the dark and the distance, she recognised fear in his taut, watchful silhouette. He is scared and hiding and right outside, right there outside the girls' division.

But it is all right. It's all right to be there in that shed. No one ever goes there. If he just stays quiet in the day no one will ever know he's there. She wishes she could tell him that no one will know. A strange, strong feeling washes over her – she would so much like to tell him it's all right. What is this feeling? Protectiveness? Comfort? The urge to comfort? She feels she could comfort because, if she has expertise in anything, it is in the matter of surviving in this school, after almost eleven years in the girls' division. She knows all about the flurry of human business that happens in and around the girls' division. But this is the most unusual thing.

She lies down on top of her bedcovers, spinning with the oddness of the boy being there and trembling with the feeling of the boy being there, and the knowledge of the boy being also wide awake and the knowledge of the boy being also scared. Suddenly, the wake-up siren goes and Lally sits up, disoriented. Somehow it is six o'clock already. She must have dropped off and slept a six-hour stretch. How singular to have slept six hours together, and in the least conducive of circumstances. She remembers the boy instantly, in the same moment of thought as the first wincing from the intrusion of the siren. She hurries over to the window, but the shed is holding its secret safely.

How can you think about biology and history when there is such a secret? She is edgy and distracted all morning, and even gentle Mrs Mackenzie has to reprimand her. By the third lesson, which is maths, Lally can't bear it anymore. She has to at least just look at the shed. She tells the maths teacher that she has forgotten her book and he gives her permission to go up to her cubicle and fetch it. As she bursts through the curtain of her cubicle, she startles the sisi who once comforted her. It is the windows day, when all the windows of the divisions and the school block are cleaned, and the sisi whips up the rag and the bottle of Windowlene that she is holding and begins to squirt and scrub. But Lally has seen already what the sisi was doing before she knew she was observed. The sisi was standing in front of the window, watching uneasily as the agricultural boys trundled their barrows between the new shed and The Plots, back and forth past the old shed with the barrows and the trowels and the rakes. The sisi tried to blank out the anxiety and gravity in her features when she heard the curtain moving on its rail behind her, and to adopt the subservient, obedient cleaner's mask that the sisis wear for the teachers and the older children. She relaxes a little when she registers that it is only Lally, but remains wary, seeming to turn her back on the window even while she is cleaning it. This departure from the sisi's usual equanimity convinces Lally that there is a connection. She is almost jubilant – it fits together: her sisi, her boy. It is like having a secret family.

She has been stationed at the window in her dark cubicle for several hours after senior lights out when the boy makes a second appearance. He goes to the log and searches under it, more lengthily than the previous night, but when he withdraws his hand it is empty and, even at this distance, she can make out the frustration and disappointment in his posture. Windows day. Lally thinks. When would the sisi have had an opportunity to pass by The Plots?

It is an irony to have unwanted porridge spooned into her bowl in the morning when a hungry fugitive crouches a few hundred yards away, and she can see from the sisi's face when she passes her en route to lessons that her failure to provide is also foremost in her mind. She thinks about the unfed boy throughout the morning and the lunch-torment and the sleepy early afternoon lessons. At teatime, a solution presents itself. Every day they get tea and jam and bread on the veranda of the girls' division, and sometimes delicacies instead, such as shortbread and rum balls, or Boston loaf. This day, and the next and the next and the next, after regular sports practice, Lally runs an extra lap around the school with the food secreted under her blouse in a fold of tissue paper. At the log, she pretends her shoelace is undone and she pokes the bundle under the wood. At first, she worries that people will notice the extra running because she has always been lazy at the compulsory practice, and she even tries to join in with the team spirit of the others, making squeaks of enthusiasm and mock-excited lunges at the netball. But afterwards she realises that on top of her usual anonymity, she is a skulker now, and if she isn't actually infringing a rule, like not eating what's on her plate, no one will care to see that she is inexplicably putting in unrequired endeavours.

So, it happens that the days now hold this sweet, unforeseen closure – the boy who comes from the shed, casts for a moment beneath a log to find a rum ball or a jam sandwich and retreats, sweeping the marks of his passage from the dust. She knows that he must be there for some stop-gap reason, and he will move on. But, for now, life has purpose. Life is waking up and seeing the shed and knowing, and then ignoring everything until teatime when she can make her delivery, and blocking all again until the senior lights out. She sits quietly in the dark between the siren for senior lights out and the boy's cautious appearance, his head venturing warily through the hole in the door like the head of one of the tortoises that live in the grassy verges along the sports fields, nudging from its shell.

He never allows himself to emerge before he has made certain that there is no one in sight, and then his time outside is very brief. But after the first couple of days he permits himself a few seconds longer, sniffing appreciatively at the night air with its grass and pineapple overtones. She guesses it must stink in the shed, with nowhere for him to bury his waste, and the hot weather coming on fast.

She attributes the boy's presence to the war-with-no-name that Pim spoke of, and she recognised, because she attributes all things that seem unpleasant and inexplicable to the war-with-no-name. It seems to her, sitting in the dark after lights out, that there must be more; more souls than her and this boy, awake in the dark hours from the perplexity of the war-with-no-name. Perhaps all over the country in sheds and cubicles and elsewhere, those who cannot fit with the war-with-no-name conceal themselves and their thoughts. This idea is enormously comforting. When the boy comes out for the jam sandwiches and the rum balls, she leans forward against the window, the task of unscrewing the screws forgotten, filled with sensations of protectiveness and kinship and the almost overwhelming feeling of having been chosen somehow to share this secret. It is like a meditation: the waiting in the dark, the suspecting of the other souls, the final indisputability of a rum ball in a boy's stomach. When the boy retreats, she sleeps, heavily and instantly.

Six days pass in this way, in watching the boy, in suspecting the presence of other souls. On the evening of the sixth day since she first saw him, she is minding the shed, waiting for him to poke through the hole, when she becomes aware of a pale blur materialising out of the darkness at the end of the boundary road between The Plots and the pineapple farm. The blur is surprisingly fast-moving, and as it approaches and becomes more distinct, she sees that it is the all-rounders, the boys-will-be-boys streakers, Preston, McGrath and Bowyer. They are running like cheetahs through the still night air, cropped heads thrown back, muscled arms and legs piston-pumping, moonlight gleaming on those pallid integrants of their skins that have not been exposed to the sun.

Lally recoils. She does not want the incursion of Preston, McGrath and Bowyer into her night vigil. She has no desire to catch them at it or take a peek at their you-know-whats. She knows she does not have much sex-feeling yet, or at least not as much as some of the other girls, who cut their eyes all day long at the boys and allow themselves to be hustled into the darker corners at dances to have their lips bruised and alarming purple raspberries planted on their necks. She is what they call 'a late developer', skinny and stringy, and only starting to menstruate in the last few months. She's never even kissed a boy, apart from that one night with Pim, to whom she gave her body. When she thinks about the time with Pim, a low heat burns in her abdomen, a gut-warmth in her stomach. She surmises that real sex-feeling emanates from somewhere lower than the stomach. But even if she was charged with sex-feeling, she would be repelled by the nakedness of Preston. McGrath and Bowyer.

At that moment, the boy's tortoise head comes poking out. His back is to the road, and though he surveys The Plots and the school, he does not look directly behind him. 'No!' mouths Lally in horror. But it is too late. He has already wriggled clear of the hole and stood up.

Preston, McGrath and Bowyer, turning their handsome heads to grin at the girls' division as they come abreast of it, all see the boy at precisely the same moment. There is a scuff of bare feet on dust as they pull up short, but they are trained cadets and drop to the ground instantly. The boy may have heard the scuff; his head turns in that direction, but he can't see Preston, McGrath and Bowyer now: they are hidden in the unmown grass at the side of the road.

The boy takes his food from under the log. He enjoys the night air for a few minutes, licking the chocolate vermicelli coating of a rum ball and urinating behind the log. Then he turns back to the shed, sighing. His body language seems to say that he is growing heartily sick of hiding in the shed, but he hasn't any choice in the matter for the moment. He hunkers on his bottom, slides through the hole, sweeps away the marks, adjusts the boards.

Preston, McGrath and Bowyer rise up from the long grass and vanish into the night.

Lally is frozen, mute and appalled at what has just happened. The first awareness to pass through her is of the pain in her hands, which are gripping the window bars. As she unclenches her hands, an almost audible voice in her head says, '*warn him!*'. Still scattered with shock, she worms her head between the loosened bars, pulling back with a sharp intake of breath as she registers the distance to the ground.

She will have to leave the building. She has never tried to leave the girls' division illicitly before and does not know of anyone else who has either. But the boys are always getting out, and the divisions are constructed along the same lines. She tiptoes down the two flights of stairs to the ground floor vestibule and tries the main entrance. It is no good – locked at three different points, and she has no idea where the keys might be.

Her ears are straining to hear the crunch of Preston, Mc-Grath and Bowyer's feet on the gravel outside. They will have to dress themselves before they call a master. She does not know how long she has, but it will not be more than ten minutes. She tries one of the other doors of the vesti-bule, but they only lead to the dining room and the ma-trons' rooms and the dormitories for the smallest children. Afraid of waking a child or a matron, she inches along the corridor to the dining room. The door to the dining room is unlocked, but the kitchen doors and the veranda doors are firmly secured and chained. She runs her hands through her hair, willing herself not to panic but rather to think clearly and quickly. Outside, every infinitesimal sound of distant vehicle or farm animal seems to translate into a har-binger of Preston, McGrath and Bowyer's return.

It comes to her – the fire escape. There is an escape door on each floor. The ground and second floor escapes lead out of dormitories, but the third floor escape is on the corridor, next to the stairs to the prefects' annexe. She pads back up the two flights and tries the lock. It gives a little, suggesting that the door might be jammed shut rather than locked. Next to the door is a key in a red box with a glass front, and in black letters on the glass front are the words BREAK

GLASS IN EMERGENCY. And suddenly Lally feels more than feels, knows – that something very bad is going to happen if she can't reach the boy first. She abandons all her caution and pulls insistently at the handle, wondering if she has the courage to just break the glass and seize the key and run into the night and deal with the consequences later.

'What are you doing, Lally?'

Lally drops the handle as if it were burning hot to the touch and whips around. Major Carlton's daughter – the new head girl – is standing halfway up the stairs to the prefects' annexe. She has cold cream on her face and rubber snakes for training curls wound into her hair, and from the way she rubs sleep from her eyes and glares accusingly at Lally, it is clear that she has been roused from her slumbers by Lally's overly noisy activities with the door handle.

'Will you kindly tell me what on earth you're up to?' Her voice is more outraged now as she emerges fully from sleep and the various possible interpretations of the situation dawn on her.

'I'm testing the fire escape.'

'Don't be ridiculous! There's never been a fire.'

'I had ... I had a feeling.' The premonition about the boy's fate is a solid, pulsing, screaming thing in her stomach.

The major's daughter's sleep-caked eyes narrow. She adopts the tone of voice reserved for skulkers.

'I believe you're fibbing, Lally. I believe you meant to bunk out.'

'I didn't! Why would I bunk out in my nightgown?'

'Are you talking back to me?'

Lally falls silent. It is a no-win situation. She is only making the cold cream and the rubber snakes angrier. She forgets about the boy for a moment and realises that she is being accused of bunking out, which will have repercussions and make her life worse than it is at the moment.

'Please,' she pleads, 'don't tell.'

'Are you asking me to break the rules?'

'No. I … no, I'm not.' Her thoughts veer wildly between priorities, and she begs: 'I have to go outside. Please let me go outside.' Major Carlton's daughter seems about to go up in smoke when she pauses unexpectedly and sighs.

'Lally. You're just more and more trouble. What will I do about you?' Her head, in its veneer of cream and styling implements shakes sorrowfully, and her features relax into an expression near sympathy. She actually quite likes Lally, despite everything that stands between them, for the series of small receptive kindnesses Lally showed her two years ago when she first arrived at the school, aching and bewildered after her mother's murder. These kindnesses have not been forgotten by the major's daughter. But you have to draw a line with the skulkers. One cannot administer discipline effectively as a prefect if one's authority is compromised by allegiances formed when one was younger and free to do as one pleased. She is not going to subvert the system that holds her family together now; that offered her father employment, that accepted herself and her sister as boarders in their hour of need, that recognised her true potential, for some odd whim of Lally's just because Lally was sweet at one time and left chocolates on a pillow.

'I have to take away your Saturday morning leave-out,' says the major's daughter firmly. 'But I won't tell matron what you tried to do. Unless …' her face grows hard again 'you don't jolly well get back into bed this instant.'

'All right,' says Lally, and, because it is expected: 'Thank you.' She goes slowly down the corridors and into her cubicle. There is nothing more she can do. Preston, McGrath and Bowyer will be there in a minute or two. She sits down dully on the chair by the window and watches the shed.

But Preston, McGrath and Bowyer do not appear in a

minute or two. A quarter of an hour passes, and then another quarter of an hour. Lally frets and chews her nails, confused. She cannot understand it. There is no reason that she can conceive of why Preston, McGrath and Bowyer would not fetch a master at once, quarry the boy out of the shed, and make an example of him for trespassing. They are certain to get lots of praise for it, and even some more tin, not that they need any more tin. It will also be a good way to let everyone guess that they pulled off the streak without their actually boasting about it themselves. Is it possible that they just felt sorry for him, and are themselves going to tell him to leave in the morning, without involving a master? But that doesn't seem likely. And the leaden foreboding still churns and revolves in her stomach.

As she is mulling over these things. sweating slightly and eyeing the shed with an obscure nervous yearning as if the structure itself will offer some solution or relief from tension, she hears the sound of a vehicle. It is not unusual to hear vehicles at night – some of the farmers like to transport their fruit and vegetables to the town in the dark so that they can load and offload in the cooler temperatures. But she knows the sound of a vehicle coming onto the school grounds – the idling of the engine as the front gates are opened, the increased gunning on the slight incline between the school block and the sports ground, the eventual scatter of gravel as the tyres hit the walks. She sees the throw of headlights before a yellow police van pulls into view around the side of the girls' division. The van cruises to the end of the gravel walk and bumps over the earthen approach to The Plots, stopping directly opposite the old shed. The headlights gleam briefly against the rusting tin walls of the shed and are switched off.

She can hear low voices intoning before they emerge. From the back of the van come Preston, McGrath and

Bowyer and two junior policemen, one of whom is carrying an axe. A third policeman waits in the driver's seat of the van. In the passenger seat is the small, unmistakable form of the brigadier. He extricates himself deftly, stepping high over the loose earth of The Plots as if he does not want to get muck on his shoes.

Preston, McGrath and Bowyer range round the shed excitedly, cadet training forgotten, as if they are part of some grand-scale *springhaasjag*. The policemen are more impassive. They watch the brigadier and wait. The brigadier smoothes his *snorretjie* with his finger and looks at the meranti door estimatingly. He nods at the axe-bearing policeman, who steps up to the door, raises the axe and gives each of the hinges a quick chop. The door falls inwards obligingly; even if the hinges are made of stern stuff, their wood-and-tin surrounds have rotted through.

The two junior policemen from the back of the van rush the shed. When they come out with the boy, his head is under one of their arms so that she can't see his face, only his hunched-over shoulders and stumbling-forward legs. In any event, they have him in the back of the van in seconds. The brigadier ventures into the shed himself. He is out again almost at once, holding his nose pinched, so that Lally sees she was correct about the boy having nowhere to bury his waste. He nods at McGrath and Preston and shakes hands with Bowyer. Then he is back in the van and the van is backing up over the earth and onto the gravel walk. The whole operation has taken under five minutes.

After the van has driven off, Preston, McGrath and Bowyer are left loitering in The Plots. They feint a few punches at each other and peer into the stinking shed and make as if they are going to push each other inside, but don't go through with it. They have an air of anticlimax and slight disgruntlement, now that the thing is out of their hands, as if they have realised too late that they would have had more personal involvement with the boy's chastisement if they had gone the less glorious route of calling a master. Despite the anticlimax, they are obviously all still too pepped-up to consider going to bed. Eventually they take a pumpkin from one of the agricultural beds, split it open on a post and throw handfuls of pumpkin at the side of the shed. By the time they finish with the pumpkin, there are orange dots all over the ground and the shed wall, and they are grinning again and in better spirits, making as if to saunter off. In the nick of time, Bowyer remembers his new responsibilities as head boy, and he makes Preston and McGrath stay and help him to pick up most of the pumpkin and artfully conceal it in the moist walls of the compost heap.

A new society

How is she to tell the sisi what happened? Because between breakfast and chapel she saw the sisi, and one glimpse of her face confirmed that the axed-in shed door has already come to her attention.

She puts up her hand at last in the third lesson, the maths lesson, and tells the teacher that she has forgotten her book. The maths teacher is her choice – not because he is the kindest one; Mrs Mackenzie is the kindest one – but because he is the least able to impose his will.

'Oh, all right, Lally,' he says, crossly. 'This is the second time in less than a week! You'll leave your head behind next.'

You'll-leave-your-head-behind-next is a standard joke, and she escapes to polite titters.

She still has to deal with matron, who is cross and more

able to impose her will. Matron stands at the bottom of the stairs and says: 'No!'

'Oh please, Matron.' She can hear movement coming from the junior bathroom at the top of the first flight of stairs. 'It's a test for trigonometric functions.' She knows matron does not have much education.

The trigonometric functions remark makes matron crosser, but takes the argument out of her territory. She gives Lally an order mark and a glare from beneath her blue rinse, but allows her to go upstairs.

Lally hurries up to the junior bathroom and throws open the door of the toilet cubicle from which the scrubbing sounds are issuing. The sisi is on her knees, bent over the toilet bowl. Lally encounters a wide semicircle of overalled bottom, indented by two broad slipper soles.

'*Sisi*!'

A head peers round. It is not her sisi.

'Where is …?' Lally realises that she does not know her sisi's name: '… the other sisi?' she finishes lamely.

'Third floor,' says the wrong sisi, resuming her scrubbing.

She sees the sisi at once at the top of the stairs. The sisi is sweeping, or making some attempt at the motions of sweeping. Her broom tamps at the floor automatically and the dust-bunnies suck and retreat with its movement but go nowhere.

'*Sisi*?' says Lally again. softly.

The sisi regards Lally. Her face is numb, blank, involuntary, as if some inner force is covering for her while her usual faculties reel.

'The boy,' says Lally.

The sisi stalls, the broom jerking in her hands, and her blankness changes to hard suspicion.

'I saw him,' says Lally.

'You told? Where is he? Where have they taken him?'

'No, I never told! I put food. But boys came. Bad boys. And brought the police, I saw. I saw it.'

The sisi pauses, searching Lally's eyes. Lally sees that she is believed, but the belief offers no relief.

'Which police?' asks the sisi, at last.

'The small one. With small hair here,' Lally touches her own upper lip, 'and he does this.' She imitates the preening movement.

The sisi drops the broom, which slides sideways into a cubicle curtain, dragging the curtain on to the bed. She sinks to her knees, letting her head fall face-down on to the bed and makes a keening, muted wail. It is not a wail of surprise. It is a wail of something being confirmed that was already suspected.

'*Sisi?*' says Lally, uncertainly. The sisi does not respond. She continues to make the unnerving crying, while crumpling her palm and driving her fist against the bed.

'Sisi, can't we … can't we ask? Someone?'

The woman looks up, sharply, and the grief of her expression is replaced by urgency.

'No! You must never say. You must never tell! This one is too dangerous.'

'Dangerous?'

'Too dangerous.' She goes back to crying, but struggles against the crying to urge Lally again. 'You must not speak about it.'

'But can't we go to the police?'

Lally realises the idiocy of her statement as soon as she has uttered it. Swallowing and frowning, she eyes the weeping servant. In all the years that she has felt lost and adrift in the world, she has never been less sure of how to deal with a situation.

'Laeticia,' Matron's voice is calling up the staircase to her, hard and angry. 'Is that you? Go back to class immediately, *this minute.'*

'Don't say,' the sisi is repeating, like a possessed person through the tears. 'Don't talk about it. This dangerous man. My other children.'

'I won't,' Lally mutters.

The next day the sisi is gone. No one knows why, although they accept that blacks have a tendency to disappear on you – from fecklessness or stabbings at the shebeen or some other regrettable quality. In any event, a replacement sisi quickly arrives.

Lally tries to ask the second sisi, the one with the wide bottom and the slippers, what happened. But the second sisi is bent on evading Lally. She is not even subtle about it. When Lally enters the room, she exits, hurriedly, obviously afraid. So Lally seeks out the new sisi. She finds her busy with the windows. It is windows day again.

'Did you know the other sisi?' demands Lally.

The new sisi's hands tighten anxiously on her rag and spray. The cleaning position, as far as opportunities for township women go, is a plum job, and she wants to hang on to it.

'What was that other sisi's name?'

The woman looks guarded.

'What was it?'

'Nomda,' says the new sisi, uncomfortably. 'Nomda Qhashane.'

'And the boy?'

'Shhhh!' The sisi glances swiftly up and down the corridor.

'Tell me!' shouts Lally. Tears spill everywhere. 'Tell me, tell me, tell me! What was his name?'

'Sipho,' says the woman at last, very quietly.

Lying awake in her bed in the night, Lally repeats the names, again and again. Nomda Qhashane. Sipho Qhashane. Nomda. Sipho. Nomda. Sipho. It is very important. It is a kind of meditation. The meditation of the names in the face of the shock makes her a little calmer at first. But the calm rapidly gives way to a kind of self-loathing. She is angry with herself, and berates herself. She has hurt herself with watching the boy because a caring came into her for him, and also a caring for his mother – the sisi. And with the caring, a need for the two of them. But it is not a safe thing in this world to make these bonds. The bonds are traps – points of vulnerability – flaws along which a stone can be cut. This world is too unpredictable, and if there are good people like Pim and the sisi, there are too many bad ones to make allowances for the good.

She should never have strayed from the chamber of ice. The reason she lost the ice chamber in the first place is because she thought she could come and go. She thought she could move between human contact and isolation. But it is not safe. She must make a commitment to the ice chamber. The moving away, the reaching out, the forays into the realm of soul-contact, which is also the world of vulnerability, are as dangerous as a lion cub gambolling out of its lair into a veld filled with predators.

It is the end of the suicide thoughts. Because suicide is a kind of engagement with the world. She would have to use the world's methods, and afterwards the world would have to clean her up and pass its judgements on her. But lying on the hot pillow in the darkness, she understands that she must close a part of herself to the world. And close it permanently. She will not be the witless cub again. She will not make the same mistakes again. She will just remain unto herself.

In the classrooms, streaking is no longer the latest joke. There is a new joke in class. The new joke follows a similar pattern to the streaking joke in that, at the beginning, it is strictly a secret joke for the popular boys who sit along the wall, but later it becomes an open joke for everybody.

The joke is about the new society. It is not really a real society, like stamp-collecting or bird-watching, but the joke grows and grows until the new not-real society has an official handshake and a logo and a membership list, and everyone wants to pretend that they were in on it from the first.

The new society is the *Society for Bashing Up Bad Kaffirs*.

Memory and Forgetting

In the photograph, police captain Jeffrey Benzien is illustrating to the Truth Commission the 'wet bag' torture
method that he used on the activists Ashley Forbes and
Tony Yengeni. Yengeni, who is now a member of parliament, has insisted on a simulation, and a volunteer has
come forward to assist. Benzien is squatting on the back of
the prone volunteer, facing the camera. He is neatly dressed
for his appearance before the commission in a three-piece
suit and a striped tie. Because he is a heavy-set man and
his belly thrusts forward as he hunkers, his stomach strains
at the buttons of his waistcoat. A stylish casual shoe – the
sort of shoe labelled in clothing chains as formal comfort
footwear – peeps from beneath the volunteer's bent-back
arm. The executive's clothes make the playground scrim-
mage position seem even odder, but Benzien's face is calm,
intent, one eyebrow raised slightly and his lips pressed together as if he is concentrating on his technique. His physical attitude evokes the succubus in the Fuseli painting who
squats on the prostrate woman, except that for onlookers
Benzien has not a hell-steed glaring through a parted curtain, but some blurred commissioners and a potted plant.

The picture is in the *Mail & Guardian*, which Pim subscribes
to, having his copies posted weekly from South Africa.

'My God,' says Pim, poring over the image. 'He looks as
if he's buggering the guy.'

Lally murmurs assent. It does look like that.

'It's unbelievable what these policemen actually did. It was
like a big, state-sanctioned murder club. I mean one knew

– sort of – that things like this happened. But to have it out in the open like this. And the extent of it!' He folds the *Mail & Guardian* again and slots it into its tube and puts the tube in his briefcase, lest he forget the paper at Lally's. As an afterthought he adds: 'What a terrific newspaper.'

'I don't think it's such a great paper,' says Lally.

'The *Mail & Guardian*?' Pim becomes proprietorial. The *Mail & Guardian* is one of his things. It constitutes his only foray into journalism, having at one time aired an excerpt from his PhD thesis as part of a larger report on the economic condition of the African subcontinent. 'It's an extraordinary paper, Lally. Clean, concise, frontline journalism. You won't find a paper in Europe that strikes its targets more spot-on.'

'It's just an ANC thing.'

'But you're so wrong!' And Pim goes into a homily about autonomous structures and journalistic ethics and the history of the *Mail & Guardian*.

She interrupts: 'I didn't mean all that. I mean right now. It's just all about the Truth Commission.'

'Well, what do you expect?' Pim allows himself to be a little vexed, also a little amused. 'It's an astonishingly significant ... no, a *seminal* event. The eyes of all the world are on this remote country at the end of Africa because we're trying – really trying – to do something big, something ∴ philosophical. We're trying to repair, Lal. To repair a country. To forge humanity!'

'I don't see the point.'

'The point?' Amusement gives way to aggravation. 'Lally – people died. Were tortured. Abducted. Families were torn apart. The most obscene things were sanctioned by people in positions of responsibility. Human beings were cooked on fires while other human beings stood around the fire drinking cans of beer. Can you understand that? That's the point. Truth is the point. Knowledge is the point.'

'Yes,' she says. 'But it doesn't make it better. It doesn't undo that it happened.'

He is about to speak again when he pauses and looks at her as he sometimes does, understanding alloyed into uneasiness, the mask of the London businessman, the confident renaissance man, slipping for a moment.

'How do you mean?'

'Because,' she explains, 'it's your memory and their forgetting. You can make yourself remember, but you can't make them not forget. So, you go there and you make yourself remember and you put yourself in that place and then ... your memory finds their forgetting. And it makes you angrier.'

He is silent, his blue eyes flickering over her face, and he swallows once. Despite the greying blonde hair, the forming neck grooves, he is her bewildered soldier-boy in the barn again.

'Pim,' she says suddenly, 'there's something – there is this one thing – I have to make a decision about something.'

Pim's cellphone rings. His body jerks and he fumbles for the plastic rectangle with its ridiculous merry screech of classical music, locating it on the faded carpet next to the futon just as it is about to switch to the messaging service.

'Hello? Edgar speaking?'

Lally can hear a rapid spin of words from the tinny secondhand voice. From the warning finger Pim holds to his lips, it must be Ruth, and she is evidently giving him a bit of a go. Pim says 'still at the office', and there are more tinny words, and Pim says 'but the switchboard's gone home, darling. I'm not going to answer the landline every time it rings – it could be anybody for anybody, I'd never finish up'. He frowns and balances the cellphone between his ear and the naked flesh of his shoulder, flexing his fingers and staring at them. Eventually he says 'about nine; nine-thirty at the latest', and there are more words and Pim says 'well, what about if I get up a bit earlier and have breakfast with him, and I'll take him through to school in the taxi and we can have a chat then? It's just a stage, I was the same way, we'll replace the damn thing'.

He hangs up and returns his attention to Lally:

'What were you saying about a decision?'

'Oh, I can't remember,' says Lally.

Preston in London

It's Monday afternoon, six months ago, and the winter has not quite broken – that uncomfortable season when you need your overcoat in the mornings and evenings, but have to carry it bundled under your arm at noon. Lally is at her work-station, Greenbow is hovering, the other agents are out with clients. The door on to Cromwell Road opens and a couple come in. Greenbow ushers them to the comfortable chairs in front of his desk. Lally is preoccupied with trying to restore some order to the directory she uses for storing flyers. Her methodical temperament prefers to make sure that each directory contains only data that pertain to its particular rubric, but Greenbow has evidently been meddling with her computer over the weekend and her flyers directory is now peppered with unlikely allusions to Greenbow's out-of-office existence such as 'wifeshop', 'tripBath', and, obscurely, considering the size of Greenbow's girth, 'gymplan'. She does not pay the couple much attention, until she hears their accents.

There are two categories of white South African accents in London – the discreetly South African, and the proud-to-be-South-African-despite-being-here-now brand. One hears the latter in the tube or Piccadilly Circus, saying things like *all these ahld buildings leave me stahn cahld*. The couple's accents are of the proud-to-be variety. The woman's intonations she can't place exactly but the man's are distinctly Eastern Cape, which makes her drum her fingers unintentionally against the desk of the work-station and crane her head to catch a glimpse of them.

'We thought Notting Hill,' the man is saying, 'or maybe Bayswater.'

The couple create an impression of largeness and stability – the man because he has a once-muscular build going visibly to fat, the shoulders still broad and powerful. The woman is only slightly taller than average, but heavily pregnant. They swell out of the comfortable chairs – two firm-foundationed, self-contained monoliths.

'Well,' begins Greenbow. 'Mr …'

'John,' interjects the other congenially, 'Let's not stand on ceremony, since we'll be working together.'

'All right, John,' says Greenbow cheerfully, jollied along by the casual approach which he always rather enjoys in the former colonials. 'What I was going to say was …' and he starts to talk about how popular Notting Hill has become in the last ten years and reels off the names of some celebrities who have made their homes there, and the pregnant wife points out that they have reservations about the carnival, and Greenbow agrees that the carnival can be seen as a detraction to the area, but he has plenty of options that are placed at such a distance from the carnival thoroughfares as to make one more or less oblivious of the proximity of the carnival, and he finishes with an anecdote about a Notting Hill friend who actually meant to go to the carnival, but didn't realise it was underway until it was over.

The couple and Greenbow sit in the comfortable chairs and smile at each other.

'We definitely need five bedrooms,' chimes in the wife. 'We've got two kids already. And even with them sharing, we need one for the au pair and one for us and one for the guests. We always have a stream of guests. And one for the nursery.' She pats her belly and beams.

'My study can double as the guest bedroom,' says John, more cautiously. 'We must observe a … uh … a price ceiling, as it were.'

'But,' breaks in the wife, and she glances meaningly at her husband, 'we're not considering anything without a garden. We need space for the kids to play, and we like to *braai* … er, cook.'

'Out of doors,' adds John, and he gives Greenbow a big, confident smile.

Lally jolts. All the while the conversation has been unfolding, she has become more and more sure that she knows the man who wants to buy a house in Notting Hill. The posture, the voice; its cadences, its resonances, its impact – everything is familiar somehow. More than familiar. Wrought-in. Etched. But John? Who is John? She does not know a John. There is no John lodged in her soul. But when the man smiles, revealing perfect teeth, recognition is instant, unmistakable. Her eyes flick involuntarily, absurdly, around the room for the other cornerstones of the triumvirate – McGrath and Bowyer.

Greenbow is still grinning away, one hand resting on the arm of his comfortable chair, one on his stomach. He knows that the sale of a five-bedroom house with a garden in Notting Hill will earn him a good, fat commission.

'Let me give you our Notting Hill catalogue,' he says. 'You can go through it at your leisure. But I have to warn you that these places are going like hot cakes.'

He turns to Lally to ask her to fetch the appropriate catalogue from the storeroom, and it occurs to him:

'Good heavens! Do you know something funny? My secretary is a South African.' Lally freezes, but Greenbow has already thrown his head back and is calling out to her in that irritating chummy way he puts on for clients to show them that they are all one big happy family here at the office, with the clients temporarily included in the bonhomie.

'Oi! Sweetpea! Come out here for a sec.'

She pushes her chair back stiffly and goes out to Preston and Mrs Preston.

'Good Lord,' exclaims Preston. 'I know you! Weren't we at school together?'

'My word,' says Mrs Preston. 'What a coincidence.'

Preston clearly cannot remember Lally's name, as he does not introduce her to his wife. However, this little piece of rudeness is lost in the moment, because Mrs Preston takes the opportunity to make a request:

'I'm afraid I have to use the little girls' room.' She makes a friendly, rueful face at Lally. 'You know what it's like when you're expecting – always dashing off to the loo.'

Lally nods vaguely. Greenbow says: 'I'll show you.' He reaches for the key, which he keeps on a hook behind his desk, despite the fact that the lavatory is not accessible to the public or anyone outside the office. One of his peculiarities is that he prefers to keep the bathroom locked, or maybe he just likes to monitor the extent of bowel-moving slacking time exercised by his employees. He leads Mrs Preston off to the toilet. Which leaves Lally alone with Preston.

'Well,' says Preston, 'fancy you being in the estate agency game.'

'I'm not. I'm just the secretary.'

'Ah, well,' he says. She can see that he is determined to be urbane, but it isn't helping that he doesn't really have much recollection of her.

'What brought you here, anyway?' he comes up with.

'My mother was born here,' she says slowly. 'I had the passport. So, I just came.'

'Oh, yes?'

This moves the conversation along to the intricacies of immigration to Great Britain, which is a fairly generic subject.

'I've been posted here by my company. We've transferred headquarters from Johannesburg and moved our primary listing to the London Stock Exchange.'

'Really?'

'Had to.' He drops his voice confidentially. 'We couldn't meet the empowerment pressure for black employees, not with any authenticity. And we're likely to attract much lower financing rates now.'

'Preston,' says Lally. 'Why did you do it?

Preston is caught off-guard.

'Do what?' he says, confused.

'Not take the blame. For throwing that cracker. That Zulu had.'

'*What?*'

'The Singapore cracker. That made Mr Payne lie on the floor, and he gave Zulu jacks for it.'

'Oh, *that!* That ridiculous thing.' He chuckles obligingly, obviously imagining that she is mock-chastising him over an old shared joke. 'All schoolboys play pranks.'

'You shouldn't have,' starts Lally. She is breaking into a chemical sweat. The words are very hard to find, and her body seems to be allowing tinctures of weird, long-ago emotions. There is a metal taste in her mouth, her heart is hammering, she needs to gulp at the insubstantial air. She does not want to ask Preston this question; she does not even want to remain in this room with him. But something drives her. This could be the only chance she will ever have to answer the most burning of questions – *why?*

She tries again.

'You should never have told … the other boy.'

'Zulu?' Preston appears genuinely helpful, in the way of a person who is trying to restrain himself from completing a stammerer's sentences.

'Not Zulu! The boy – the black boy – who was hiding in the tin shed! You saw, and you told.'

Preston looks bemused. Then the light dawns and the befuddled expression is replaced by one of tolerant amusement, which he tries unsuccessfully to conceal.

'You're talking about that vagrant.'

Lally makes a wordless movement with her head, between a nod and a shake.

'I didn't even think that had got out. The headmaster didn't want the lady matrons twittering on about security.'

Greenbow is heard returning from his tour of duty to the toilet. Preston says gently, patronisingly:

'Of course we weren't going to let a vagrant loiter there.' He remembers now exactly who the girl was – the quiet one who was friends with Zulu and sat in the desk across from the girl who was a bit of a porker.

Preston prides himself on his people skills. He has done a series of motivational and teamwork courses with the company and he can tell from the body messages that this secretary is giving off that it is time for a supportive you-statement.

'You're kind-hearted,' he tells her. 'You've got compassion. It's a good quality. You mustn't lose that.'

Greenbow says: 'Here's the catalogue,' holding it out. Preston accepts it. Lally is still standing silently next to the comfortable chairs. They wait for Mrs Preston. By way of conversation, Preston remarks to Lally, seriously:

'Of course, there was hardly any problem with vagrancy then, compared to now.'

'I've heard as much,' agrees Greenbow. 'Terrible problems with crime you have over there.'

'Shocking,' confirms Preston. 'I wasn't sorry to get out of Johannesburg, I can tell you that. Never had a minute's peace of mind about my wife.'

Greenbow makes a sympathetic humming sound. Mrs Preston comes back. The Prestons drape their coats, which have been hanging on the backs of the chairs, over their large bodies. As they are leaving, Preston remembers at last the secretary's name, and something else.

'Lally!'

Her head jerks up: 'Uh?'

'Weren't you mates with Pim and that lot?'

She mumbles – yes, she was.

'You in touch with Pim?'

She mumbles again – no, she's not.

'They're in London. Not the whole family – just Pim, but he's married, terrific girl apparently. His mum saw mine and gave her his details, and I've been meaning to get in touch, but you know how it goes. You can get in touch for me; I've got the number in my Filofax.' He writes it down on a Post-it, which Greenbow obligingly supplies, and holds the Post-it out to Lally. 'Give him a call, why not? Us exiles have to keep the home fires burning.' He looks pleased to have been able to furnish her with a contact. 'All right, bye, Tim, thanks a lot. Bye, Lally.'

And out they go onto Cromwell Road.

Lally looks at the door. The panic which had begun to assail has vanished. What is left is a dull throbbing ache and a low, ominous rumbling in her belly.

Greenbow is still gloating. He says absently to Lally:

'Nice people.' She can tell that he is pleased with her for the useful sense of fellowship she has helped to create, which will almost surely result in a sale.

'Mr Greenbow – I think I'm going to go home. I don't feel very well.'

He looks up sharply but remembers that she has never yet asked for time off and becomes solicitous.

'You *are* a little pale.'

'My stomach,' she says. 'Ate something nasty.'

Greenbow tut-tuts feelingly. Being what he likes to describe as an adventurous gourmet, he has a near professional interest in the subject of discommoded stomachs.

She takes her coat from the peg and goes outside. The late afternoon air is crisp and chill and, remarkably for London, the sky is quite cloudless, the winter light keen, crystal-blue and unflawed. Ordinarily, she might resent this mysterious weather because she does not like what she can't explain, but now the sheer bite of it is good, because her habitual numbness has left her. She hurries along the less frequented streets between Cromwell Road and Holland Road, past the streaky bacon edifices, sucking at the raw air, willing herself to make it home. At her house, the ever-present medical experimentees are installed on the stairs. She pushes past and hustles up to the top-floor bathroom, where she falls on her knees, flips up the mottled toilet lid and sicks up.

Sitting back on her haunches, she wipes her mouth on the topside of her hand, gasping, a compromised figure in this unpromising bathroom with its specked mirror, mould-based chipped enamel bath and naked bulb on a flex that swings when people tread the floorboards.

The thought of Preston returns and she is sick again. The retch is thin and colourless because she does not usually eat until the evening. With her head over the toilet bowl, she wills viscerally the house in Notting Hill to fall down and smash them all to pulped oblivion – Preston, Mrs Preston, the children, the foetus, the stream of guests.

She straightens up, which presents her instantly with a mirrored vision of her own face. She stares at the face. It is bright red. She is in a fury. *I'm in a fury.* Tears stand in the corners of her eyes – from the force of the retching, from pain, from anger? *I want to kill him.* She covers her face with her hands, pressing hard. When she takes them away there are funny little crescents of blood against the red skin of her cheeks and she can't understand it until she looks at her palms and sees that she has ripped them with her fingernails.

One of the medical experimentees comes and knocks on the door. The bulb on its cord swings gently.

'Are you puking? I gotta take a leak!'

'Go fuck yourself,' says Lally.

Going Away

Lally is seventeen-and-a-half when she writes her matric exams. She gets As in English and history, Bs in biology, geography, Afrikaans and mathematics. It's a good result, adequate – more than adequate – to get her into university. Her parents would struggle to put her through university (ostrich farming never really survived the invention of the car, whose breezier exhilarations led to the abandonment of large feathers in hats). But Lally applies for, and is awarded, a teaching bursary.

Just before she writes her exams, she gets a windfall. A godfather in England (who she never knew) has died and left her a thousand pounds. A thousand pounds is a lot of money. It has come at a good time. Lally's mother tells Pim's mother, it will allow her comforts at university that she would have gone without otherwise.

When Lally hears about the money, she grows meditative and, all the time that she is doing well in the subjects of English, history and biology, she is making mental plots and calculations that have little to do with the comforts available at university. When the exams are over, she tells her mother that she is going to Europe for a few months. Her mother is not pleased. It is profligate, she tells Lally, and you are too young to go alone.

'But I've always been alone,' says Lally.

The child is obdurate, stony, unrelenting, and it wearies her mother to try to contend with her. Also, it seems, distressingly, that the time for mothering is past without having been comprehensively entered into. Nevertheless, a battle is waged. Lally sends away for a passport, but when the package arrives in the post office box in town, Lally's mother appropriates it and locks it away in her bureau. Lally says nothing but, when the servant sounds the gong for lunch, she is nowhere to be seen.

'She'll eat when she's hungry,' advises Lally's father, which proves untrue. Days go by and there is a song of air in Lally's ears, an ethereal sensation of imminent victory.

'You're being most unfair,' her mother complains. Lally shrugs. Fair and unfair are just words. The only thing that matters is will; will and comprehension.

One day, the song of air is an opera and she falls into a swathe of long grass beside the ostrich pens, where a farm worker finds her and reports it as a snake bite. In hospital, there is a drip in her arm, a fat Afrikaans matron, a coloured under-sister, a posy of everlastings in a glass jar. A day later, the package is on her bedside table and a sour, defeated expression on her mother's face.

As Lally waits in the airport for her flight, a tremendous map-of-the-world feeling grips her. It persists on the aeroplane all the way to London and throughout her first month in Europe. Intoxicated by the feeling, she sees Big Ben, the Tate, the Tower and, in Paris, the Louvre, the Arc de Triomphe. She sits on stone benches in public parks with the leaves blown off the trees – bare branches outlined against curdling grey skies – eating wads of bread and ham (it is the one time in her life that she eats voraciously) and being careless and invigorated.

In the second month, this intoxicated state subsides. A new, more complicated condition comes over her. If the old feeling was a form of joy, this one is more like depression. It needles her, pointing always towards her future – purposeful and bleak. She tries to hold on to the unthinking excitement, but the new doubts relentlessly shoulder their way in.

'What now?' the new feeling seems to say. 'What do you want to do?'

I'm going to university. Pim has already been at university in Cape Town for two years. When she sees him, she asks – what is it like? You meet a lot of people, he says, from different backgrounds. Gentle is a word he has used several times to describe it, looking at his hands. He works sedulously – even in the holidays he is always in his room with his books and papers – and he has been awarded the class medal for both years.

And after university she will be qualified to be a schoolmistress. She will get some job at a day school in a city somewhere.

Sometimes she sees other South Africans. She recognises them by their insistent, braying voices and their obsession with the weather conditions. Mostly they are older than her, but still young, and she supposes they must have made decisions. Hoping to glean a chance word or reference that might illuminate, she lingers on the borders of their conversations, but they are empty and she can't learn anything.

In the youth hostels she stays in, she finds Europeans and Americans. They come from Berlin, Rome, Boston, Detroit. She listens attentively to the stories of the Berlin-Rome-Boston-Detroit worlds, which are so different from her own world. When the Europeans and Americans find out where she is from, expressions of self-conviction and moral outrage enter their faces and they move away from her. A few sidle closer with complicit racist comments and masks of sympathetic understanding. So, after a while she modifies her accent to a kind of generalised white African brogue and if people ask where she is from she says Zambia or Botswana or Lesotho.

In the third month, she defines two choices for herself. She can be a citizen, or she can be an activist.

Being a citizen will mean shutting herself down, shutting down her faculties – sealing her eyes, ears, mouth, mind – blundering as obtusely as possible through whatever is thrown at her – studentship, schoolmistressing, marriage. It will be a pretence; but life is always a pretence.

The idea of being an activist is less clear. She knows indistinctly that there is a category of white women, *those terrible unnatural women*, who help to perpetrate violence, who operate somehow in a way that is destructive to the state. The name Ruth First is in her mind. She does not know who Ruth First is or what she does, but she knows from the way the name Ruth First is said, when it is said at all, that Ruth First is one of the insurrectionists.

But where would you even find the insurrectionists? At a university, she supposes. It would be more likely than at any other place. She tries to visualise herself at university – accepted, trusted and trained by other insurrectionists – and instead of schoolmistressing, putting bombs in strategic places. It is difficult to imagine.

There is a third choice, and it is the choice she finally makes, although perhaps it is more of a default than a choice, and it seems to choose her more than she chooses it. At the end of her three months, she phones British Airways to confirm her flight home. In the afternoon, she packs her rucksack in the dormitory of the youth hostel. She leans the rucksack against the iron leg of the bed and goes out for a walk, up Earls Court Road towards Hyde Park. There is an end-of-winter hush overlying the park; the frigid, brown water in the ponds, the fluffed-up ducks, the stiff blades of grass scruffy with tramped-in sleet. The pale-grey clouds dull into pewter and then schoolsock-grey and a park van motors up to her and the park warden advises her that the gates are closing shortly.

In the evening, she gets quite drunk with two Australians. They wander up and down the pavements outside the youth hostel and throw fragments of tar and grit at the hubcaps of passing cars. She goes up to the dormitory very late and collapses fully clothed on top of the bedding, although she does remember to set the alarm clock before she falls asleep. At six o'clock, its mechanical blurted beeps alert her. She rolls over in the bed and frowns at the luminous face of the clock, chewing on her thumb.

'Turn it off, fa Godsake,' moans a sleeper in an adjacent bed. 'Middle of the fuckin' night.'

She turns it off. She sleeps for a long time. When she wakes up, she unstraps her rucksack and takes her folded towel out of the inner compartment. In the shower, she lets the warm trickle spool over her head and shoulders. She dries herself and dresses.

Towards lunchtime she goes into the large room at the core of the youth hostel that is used as a common room. Lying on the table in the centre of the room are a couple of editions of magazines for young people and travellers that have housing lists in them. She picks one up and pages through it, thinking that it will be more economical to live in a shared house than a youth hostel.

Lovers and Children

Ruth's pregnancy has been successfully achieved.

'Irrevocable,' says Pim half-ruefully, although he is rapidly adjusting to the idea of a third child. He has dropped in to see Lally on the way back from work again. It has become quite a regular twice-a-week routine to see Lally here in her little attic bedsit or in the square of garden outside. Tonight, on his way up the stairs, a swarthy young man coming down from the bathroom on the top floor saw him and called out playfully, 'Ciao, playboy'.

Some of the medical experimentees moved on and were replaced by a group of artists from Venice, who paint and eat and make love and a lot of noise all in a huge bare room on the ground floor. Sometimes Pim and Lally have fun with the artists, getting drunk in the garden in the early evenings. Pim brings bottles of ramazotti and chianti and slices of prosciutto from the expensive Italian shop in Fulham, which makes him popular. He likes getting drunk in the garden and being teased by the artists – it makes him feel young again. But they're not getting drunk tonight as he was unable to come up with a watertight excuse and are sitting alone on a ramshackle bench under a beech tree at the far end of the lawn. Pim feels disconsolate because there isn't enough time to do anything fun, and his life is chopped up into bits and accounted for, and he's forty and the weather is getting colder. A thought strikes him, not for the first time,

'Didn't you ever want to have kids, Lal?'

'No, I didn't.'

'Oh, you must have. Women do   they become *pressed.*'
Pim likes to sound vague and thwarted by the operations
of female biology, despite having attended the births of
both his sons and weathered the storm of a miscarriage
with Ruth, and, before that, a number of pregnancy scares
with various parties. But being vague makes him feel safe-
guarded from the hotter impositions of gynaecology.

Lally considers. She wouldn't say that she felt pressed. In
fact, the whole notion of mothering fills her with a kind of
nonspecific uneasiness. She did once think she was pregnant because she missed two periods. She was twenty-one.
The person she thought had made her pregnant was an
Israeli originally from Yemen, a man called Nir, who was
almost unnaturally beautiful. A mole-lover, she thought
him in his thrusting insistence in the sheets, his brown
velveteen skin and river-water eyes. She was working on a
kibbutz as a potato-picker and Nir was the potato-picker
overseer. But his passion, apart from women, was grapes.
He liked to use grapes in a kind of after-play, tearing off the
skin with his teeth and tonguing out the pips before pushing the prepared fruit from his mouth into hers. She wasn't
the first South African woman he had slept with. He never
knew her very well, but he knew her kind.

'Ah hah,' he joked, sappy with grape juice. 'What would
your mother say about me? Black *and* Jewish!'

She frowned against the mention of her mother. But the
idea of being pregnant by Nir was both appalling and en-
ticing; a future of bringing up the baby on the kibbutz,
sealed off effectively from any return to her past. Except she
did a test and it came back negative, and the Israeli doctor
told her she had amenorrhea because she was underweight
and prescribed a protein shake, and then, perhaps because
of the protein shake or all the grapes, her period returned
with her next cycle.

She slept with one other black man, a Nigerian student called Arthur who was doing a master's degree in development at the School of Oriental and African Studies. Arthur was different to Nir. Although he also reminded her of a mole, but for different reasons. A kind man, prematurely professorial, his eyes anxious and obscured behind National Health spectacles, Arthur was a storyteller, which she liked. He told her about his home, his mother and his sisters, fussy kissing aunts and obese patriarchal uncles. His boyhood, bicycling around the streets of Lagos, stealing mangoes from the neighbours' tree and being whipped for it by a sorrowful, head-shaking father. Boarding school in England, lonely and foreign at first, later stimulating.

After a time, he tried to pry out her stories. She told him about potato-picking and other incidents of travel, summers in Europe, pompous bosses. But he wanted to know before that – their common heritage of Africa.

'I don't remember,' said Lally.

'But you must. What was it like?'

'I don't recall. So long ago.'

'Were you a good child, or were you naughty? Tell me your escapades.'

'I can't remember.'

'Well, your town, at least. Describe that.'

'Small,' she said. 'Hot in the summer.' Big, Small. Hot. Cold. She found general words.

He realised she was faking and evading. As they grew closer, he became professionally worried about her.

'You need to sort things out,' he told her.

'Sort what out?'

'You're not the only one,' he said, 'to be confused. To be angry.'

Arthur's father, a lawyer, and Arthur by association, had become prey in Nigeria. However, Arthur had not given up on Africa. He wanted her to marry him, to go back to South Africa with him. The unbanned ANC was consolidating its position and certain to win the coming elections. She was at an age where women think of marriage, and she found herself attracted to the idea. The financial and emotional security of being an academic's wife. A little house in Cape Town. A child. She could even take a degree herself. She let her mind gyre around these fantasies. Gentle suburban evenings, a living room banked with books, Arthur bent over a pile of papers, groaning at some student's idiocies. Lally cooking pasta in the evenings, or Nigerian dishes which Arthur would teach her to make. Arthur in an apron, fumbling with squares of salted fish.

But in the end his insistences and solicitations infuriated her. The words he used.

'You have got to negotiate these *blockings,* Lally. You have got to own the past.'

He made her past into a piece of theory. Or sometimes her future.

'Africa needs people like us.' Excited and idealistic behind his spectacles. 'To go back. To believe.' Lally didn't see how Africa, or anything else for that matter, could possibly need her.

'Just leave me be,' she railed at him. 'Just leave me, Arthur. Just leave me alone.'

Until he did.

Dinner with Mark

Mark is visiting Ruth and Pim in the aftermath of his divorce.

'He would like to see you,' says Pim to Lally. She laughs. But Pim, it appears, is not making a joke.

'Ruth mentioned to him that you were living in London and he wants to catch up with you. You'll have to come to dinner with us again.'

She stares at him, appalled.

'Are you mad, Pim? In your house? With Ruth? I can't do that.'

'You can't not do it. He's asked me several times – in front of Ruth. It'll look more suspicious if you don't come.'

'Ruth must have some idea,' mutters Lally.

'Of course she doesn't. She thinks you're an old family friend.' Pim's tone is wearied and indignant, but really Lally does exhaust him sometimes. 'I wouldn't be so stupid as to jeopardise my marriage. Do you think I would be here if she knew?'

That strikes both of them simultaneously as being rather shallow and they glower at each other.

'You're a real prince, Pim,' says Lally, and resigns herself. Nevertheless, she feels obligated and resentful because she has to endure a ridiculous situation on account of some odd whim of Mark's, whom she barely knows any longer. She's seen him perhaps half a dozen times since he was a small boy.

She leaves her bedsit intending to catch a bus to Pim's house, but the bus arrives almost instantly at the stop and the thought of being inserted into the Pim domestic situation in less than fifteen minutes is unpleasant. It's been raining lately but is not now so she elects to walk. The summer is definitely over, with a nip in the air and the leaf edges curling brown on the trees, crackly and precarious on drying stems. Overhead, the first spearheads of birds.

'It's so boring,' she says aloud and kicks petulantly at a snapped-off twig on the pavement. This morning, she looked in the minor and saw a thread of inadequately wiped-off lipstick had worked its way into a fissure running down from the corner of her mouth. She swabbed at the offending streak from a vial of Clinique, feeling distressed and old. Although, when she glanced at herself later in the mirror in the office bathroom she couldn't see anything significant.

'Hello, Laeticia,' greets Ruth, who opens the door, with almost a glad quality in her voice which surprises Lally. Lally returns the greeting. It's difficult to imagine that the house was a seat of erotic passion only weeks before, with the scattered Lego in the passageway and the two small green mackintoshes still damp from yesterday's squall.

'Edgar and Mark are in the garden with the boys,' explains Ruth. 'Do go out. I just have to brown the potatoes.'

What Ruth calls the garden is really not much more than a yard, a square of tiles and potted shrubs leading off from the conservatory. The younger son is pushing a plastic motorbike around the perimeter and the older son is squeezed against Pim on the bench. Mark is leaning against the fence smoking a cigarette.

'We had real bikes when we were children,' says Mark, although his Eastern Cape accent makes the word come out as *barks*. 'We were fuckin' horrors on them.'

'Can I have a proper motorbike, Daddy?' begs the older son.

'We were on a farm, scamp,' says Pim. 'There's nowhere you could ride a motorbike here.'

'There's nothing kids can do here,' contends Mark bellicosely. 'Turning them into poofters.'

It is unclear whether he means London children in general or just Pim's two.

'Hello, Mark,' says Lally, emerging from the conservatory door. Mark heaves himself off the fence and kisses her, hard and directly on the mouth, so that his stubble leaves a slight burn on her chin. He has a strong natural smell rather like the odour of grass after rain, tinctured with aftershave. He is good-looking in an ordinary, beer-advertisement way – a clean, defined look – with cropped hair the colour of the veld in winter and symmetrical, delineated cheekbones.

Do you offer condolences about divorces, or just not refer to them? It seems artificial not to mention it, especially since she was at the wedding, which coincided with her last visit home.

'How have you been?' she asks cautiously.

'All right. Thrown out of my home and livelihood by a crazy cunt, but otherwise can't complain.'

'Ah,' says Lally. Pim is less than delighted about having the term 'crazy cunt' deployed in front of the boys, but unsure of how to point this out without drawing their further attention to it.

'Mark,' he ventures unhappily, picking at his fingernail, 'we do try to keep the tenor of the conversation – well, something less than blue.' He nods in the direction of the boys, who are now playing together with the bike.

Mark becomes avuncular.

'Great little fuckers,' he says pleasantly to Lally. 'Got one myself.' And he has got his wallet out and is rifling through his bank cards to find a photograph.

'Oh, how sweet,' says Lally. 'How old?'

'Three.'

'Four,' corrects Pim. 'He's older than our little one. Ruth was just pregnant at the christening.'

'Ja, that's right,' Mark's face clouds over. 'Wasn't allowed to see him on his bloody birthday, was I?'

Ruth appears, wiping her hands on a dish towel, and asks if Pim will set the table and wash the boys' hands as supper is nearly ready. Lally is left alone with Mark who, looking after Pim, is making a dog-choking-on-a-collar gesture.

'Poor bastard,' he says. 'Still, s'pose he had to marry her.'

Lally doesn't understand. The older boy was born a year into the marriage.

'Nah, passport.' Mark sniffs disdainfully, staring off into the crepuscular skies where banks of rain clouds are gathering again, seeming so low and dense that the chimney-pots are stilts holding up a roof of sky. 'Seventh generation sap like he is.' He looks at his photograph again before replacing it in his wallet, and the wallet in his pocket and lights another cigarette, drawing on it reflectively. 'Bonus of my current situation is that I'm free to do the same.'

'You want to live here?' says Lally faintly. Impossible to visualise that wild-dog body prowling to a desk job in the City of a morning, stopping at Sainsbury's for a pot noodle on the way home.

'Well, the countryside, maybe. I was a good farmer.' There is an oblique, vulnerable shift in his features and she suddenly sees a shadow of the child who ran over the lawns in his bare feet and dressing gown to crouch at Major Carlton's booted feet.

'We're all going to have to get out sooner or later, aren't we,' says Mark.

Ruth has made a roast chicken and potatoes, mangetouts, baby carrots, Brussels sprouts and a mixed salad. Mark warms to his theme over the course of the meal.

'Mate of mine,' he says to Pim, 'from Zimbabwe, right? Family decided to stay after eighty-one, give the Afs a chance, *see* what happened. Bugger got his main farm designated last year. Muggins left him a fuckin' holiday place they had in Chinoyi – that's all, about ten hectares – nothing they can farm on that. Bugger's leaving for New Zealand now, but he doesn't have a brass farthing to start up with. Says if he knew at Independence what he knows now, he would have got out first chance.'

Pim makes a non-committal noise. Ruth is helping to carve the younger son's serving of chicken breast into smaller pieces. The older son leans his elbows on the table and says:

'Uncle Mark, I'm doing a school project on great figures in history.'

'Thing is,' says Mark, 'when you left I thought you were a fuckin' wanker. Thought you weren't prepared to make a stand. And so did Dad. Well, you know. Didn't speak to you for months.'

'I've chosen David Livingstone.'

'But you were doing the right thing. The farm's unsalable. Stock thieves like rabbits. And if you shoot the bastards, you're up for murder.'

'I didn't leave because I was unprepared to live under the ANC,' says Pim rather rigidly, 'I left originally because I had the opportunity to study. And I've stayed because this is where my wife belongs.'

'Ja,' says Mark sarcastically. 'Right.'

Ruth winces. She makes an inarticulate, protesting sound as if preparing to say something more definite, but at that moment the boy interjects:

'I think David Livingstone's a great figure in history because ...'

'Shut the fuck up,' Mark shouts. 'Don't they learn you in

school to keep your mouth shut?'

Ruth gasps. The boy's eyebrows lift and he considers Mark wordlessly, his round blue eyes filming with tears.

'Jesus, Mark,' Lally hears herself saying, 'He's a little child. He's just trying to tell you about something he's interested in.'

Mark's chin is pulled back into his neck in an exasperated, don't-push-me-any-further posture. His grey eyes move from Lally to Pim to Ruth and he shrugs, shaking his shoulders into a more relaxed position.

'Sorry, Pim, but they piss you off when they're still running around this time of night.' The continuing silence at the table leads him to think that further apology might be required, so he adds in an aside to Ruth, forking a mouthful of chicken and sprouts up to his jaw, 'Must be damn difficult to cope without proper servants.'

'We have a very reliable au pair,' says Ruth icily. 'We don't expect her to work in the evenings.' She pushes back her chair and goes through to the kitchen, taking the younger son with her on her hip and telling the older son to bring through the dirties.

Lally's chair is nearest to the entrance to the kitchen. She suddenly feels very tired, more than a physical tiredness, a kind of blinding hopeless fatigue. In the kitchen, Ruth is attempting to mollify her son by asking him an endless stream of questions about his project.

'The best ones are going to be on display for open day,' enlarges the boy nasally, since he is now in the midst of a delayed-shock snivel.

'And yours is sure to be one of them,' surmises Ruth loyally, administering the dish towel.

'Mate of mine,' Mark says to Pim, capturing Lally's attention again. 'Top Johnny on a construction site. Government project, so he can't hire who he wants to for labour.

Just gets given these affirmative actions. Voters, you know. Big crowd sitting around picking their noses. Only time they get off their arses is to rob him blind. Every morning he's down at the site and there's nothing left. Cement, tools, mixers – gone. *Voertsek*. Night watchman swears he saw nothing. Course he can't fire the fucker because he's unionised. When the government bloke arrives and sees there's nothing happening, my mate tells him the straight truth – these voters are all in on it, every last one – there's nothing I can do. Goes home and what does he get? Death threats to him, his wife, his kids, for being a racist.'

'Mark. Let's talk about something else,' says Pim.

'What else, *boet*? What the fuck else is there to talk about?'

In the kitchen, Ruth is saying to her older son: 'Darling, put your jammies on and do your teeth and help Tootie with his jammies and teeth and I'll be up in five minutes.'

'Can we sleep with you and Daddy?'

'No.' But the younger son, who has been stonily silent since the Mark outburst, is looking at her with imploring eyes and she relents.

'Oh, all right … but just for tonight.'

Ruth comes back into the dining room for another load of plates. Lally makes a move to get up and help, but Ruth waves her down. Lally feels she would rather be in the kitchen, but since she's pinioned here, she might as well get drunk. Mark is already drunk and, as he gets drunker, moves erratically between his political perceptions and the chaos of his personal life.

By the time Pim breaks the seal on the next bottle of sauvignon, in Mark's head the terrorist president and his jail-trash henchmen have leagued together to keep him from seeing his son. Pim is keeping up a repetitive routine of 'Mmm. Uh-huh. Ja, Mark', waiting for ten o'clock, when he can reasonably excuse himself and go to bed.

Lally can hear Ruth moving about upstairs. *I'm screwing your husband, you stupid bitch.* Domestic Ruth with her soft brown hair, put on your jammies, do your teeth, you can sleep with Daddy and me. Ruth with her pretty-puppy, late-adolescent face, her soft, posh home counties vowels. I was fucking your husband in a barn on a farm twenty years ago when you were a little butterfly in a straw hat, a little English rose getting a rosette at a church bazaar, doing your pony club in your jodhpurs and your hard hat, holding mummy's hand, mugs of cocoa and *Just William* stories in your English bed in your mild summer English evenings, in your cold English winter nights, your school fairs, your garden fêtes, your cautious, undemanding Saturday afternoon strolls on rolling downs. I was fucking a part of your sad soldier-husband you can't even begin to suspect. And she's so jealous, nailed into her chair across the table from angry Mark, from exhausted Pim, so bloodily viscerally jealous of Ruth. Not because Ruth has Pim, but because Ruth has a past like a Merchant-Ivory film. How could Ruth not be a good mother with her milky-breath past, her crumbling cookies and hat-ribbons childhood? And how could Lally even begin to know how to treat a child? What could she ever have learnt about the gentler rhythms of life in an institution, in an institution that was part of an institution, a layering of institutions, one on top of the other? She would have wanted to have a marriage, she would have wanted to have a child, if she had come at it from Ruth's position. But what has she got? *What do I really have?*

'Course if you're black you can rape and murder 'til you're blue in the face,' Mark is saying. 'But a white Christian man like me can't have a private argument with his wife without the law breathing down my neck.'

There are a couple of soiled side-dishes left on the table. Lally picks them up and carries them through to the kitchen. Ruth has finished with the children and resumed the washing-up, bent over the sink, her small embonpoint frame rather hunched.

'Ruth,' says Lally.

Ruth turns a blotchy, tear-stained face.

'Oh, Ruth,' says Lally.

'I can't bear him,' whispers Ruth soggily. 'I know I should try to love him but I just think of what he did to that poor woman and I can't bear him.'

'I can't either,' comforts Lally. 'He was a dreadful small boy, and he's a worse adult.'

'It's not just him.' Ruth sniffs a couple of times in rapid succession, her eye anxiously on the kitchen entrance. 'It's South Africa in general. It should be a second home for me because of Edgar and I don't … it's not easy to … it seems so … rough. The farm. And Edgar's family.'

'But Michael is a lovely man,' reminds Lally. 'And Caroline is very kind.' Although Aunt Caroline was hardened by the death of Ross, especially years later when it ceased even to be heroic.

'Ye-es,' agrees Ruth, sounding unconvinced. Her mouth tugs down at the corners again. 'I'm just so afraid that Edgar might want to go back some day. I mean for good. To go home.'

'Pim will never go back,' says Lally with certitude.

Running Away

'You're running away, Lally,' says Pim. 'You've been running for so long you don't even know how to stop.'

It's not the first time he has initiated this kind of discussion. Usually she responds defensively and hyperbolically, with a poetic streak that comes over her when she's angry:

'Do *I* connive at being English? Do *I* eat tea cakes with delicate fingers, and wax rhapsodic about regency furniture?' and they have a row about identity.

But this time she only says: 'I know I am, Pim. But you ran away too.'

'I ran towards,' says Pim.

Lally in Brighton

She will write a letter. She will sit in this café off the narrow lanes of this raffish historic town of funfair rides and rock candy that was once famous for the medicinal benefits of sea-swimming, and she will write the letter. This is what she thought as she searched her London room for the things that could jog her memory. This is what she thought as she boarded the blue-and-white train with the dirty plush seats at Victoria Station. This is what she thought as she got out beneath the Victorian arches and walked through the town centre and loitered awhile on the stony beach with its polluted wash of water under the pier. And came to this restaurant, with a view of the street and ordinary people going about ordinary lives. She thought – *I will write a letter and I will be done with it.*

But it is not the easiest thing to write a letter. The question is – where to start?

She looks up from the blank sheet of onion-skin paper. It is a small café; dark, anonymous, rectangle-shaped. Opposite is the counter. The specials are chalked in gaudy colours on boards that hang on the walls. Behind the counter are the grill and the fridges and the preparation table – in open view, which she likes, given her delicacy about food. There are seven or eight round tables, flanked by chairs, and at the far end of the restaurant the door to the bathrooms with Victorian silhouettes of a man and a woman to show the way. A picture window looks out on the street, but it has a tint, allowing her to see out although those outside cannot see in, which is also pleasant. She has chosen a seat next to the window and ordered a coffee.

The waiter brings the coffee and warm milk. She adds the milk and sips at it, aware of the hot, bitter flavour, the waiter's immediate loss of interest as he resumes his banter with the cook, the sheet of paper in front of her.

What was the start of things?

But her gorge rises up, and she leans back suddenly against her chair, fighting the old nausea, the old feeling of coercion. You can't just storm to the start. If you have to return, it is better to inch your way back slowly, circumspectly, along the routes that were at least of your own choosing.

She tastes the coffee again, reaches into her handbag and pulls out a square parcel. The parcel contains photographs – all her photographs. She has never owned a camera, but now and then photographs come her way. There are about fifty, not in an album, but protected from dust and moisture by a folded square of cotton. The square of cotton is held in place by two rubber bands which criss-cross each other. They are organised in a rough chronology, not so much by design as by the fact that she tends to add them to the pile as she gets them and then not look at them again. She is not a photograph person.

Lally eases the rubber bands off the cotton-clad parcel; lays them aside and smoothes out the cotton, exposing the little pile. The top photograph is of Greenbow, his two assistants and Lally. They have the slightly drunk, bored look of attendees at a corporate function, apart from Greenbow, who is smirking in such a way as to suggest that he is surmising ways of making money. The photograph was taken four months ago, she sees from the digital orange date on the bottom of it. She can't remember what the function was or who took the photograph but supposes it must have been another estate agent. This hypothesis is confirmed when she lifts up the Greenbow photograph and puts it face-down on an unused part of the cotton, revealing a picture of herself standing beside a corpulent middle-aged man, which jogs her memory so she recalls it was an industry networking event and Greenbow pestered the whole office into going. She wonders briefly how lonely and friendless this stranger must be, to send copies of photographs to people who know and care nothing about him, except insofar as he might prove a useful contact.

The next few photographs are a scramble of the various things she has done in her early thirties – a cut-price skiing holiday in Slovakia with an Australian girl she was friends with at one time, and there they are in Australia itself, with Ayers Rock in the background. A diving holiday in Eilat – Lally has clinging wet hair and looks chilly, glancing over her shoulder at the photographer as she tries to struggle out of a wetsuit. Afterwards she went to Egypt, and there she is next to a camel, neither of them looking very impressed with the other. Many holidays, many diversions.

A few pictures down, she finds one of her and a few other people in a youth hostel in Amsterdam. It must have been sent to her some time after it was taken, because she knows she was only twenty-nine the last time she was in Amsterdam. She scrutinises the image. Her expression interests her. It is dry, at odds with the gaiety of the others, the American kids, sitting at the Formica tables of the youth hostel refectory in a cloud of pot. American kids with studs in their tongues. The boy on her left was her lover for a few days. She cannot remember his name – one of those American names that sound more like surnames. All she can remember about him is that he ejaculated too quickly but didn't seem aware of it, or embarrassed by it, and she recalls being frustrated, sexually, and resentful about the lack of embarrassment. It seems a sadly inadequate recollection to constitute the summation of a human life.

But perhaps she seems detached because they are all stoned and she isn't. She can't smoke pot because it gives her paranoid hallucinations. She did push it periodically when she was younger, wanting the laughter, the loose limbs, the abandoned release other people seemed to achieve. But she has not tried anything psychotropic or hallucinogenic for fifteen years. Or perhaps she seems other than them because it was at this time of her life that she began to yearn, quite strongly, after normality, consistency. In the years after leaving South Africa, the travelling was everything – a whole identity; a lifestyle. But in her late twenties it began to feel fictitious. A cover-up. Not enough. As her thirtieth birthday approached, she thought she would try again, really try, to make a settled life. So, she went back to London, and it worked at first. She met Arthur almost immediately. And was happy, more or less. But Arthur came unravelled and she was on the hoof again. Knowing that travelling in your thirties is different to travelling in your twenties.

On cue, the Arthur pictures surface, Arthur before Amsterdam, although in life it was the other way round. There are quite a few Arthur pictures, because Arthur had a camera and an academic's zest for documentation. One shows a young man, close-cropped tight curls, glinting glasses, very earnest, a bare coffee-coloured arm extended to butter a biscuit as he kneels in front of an orderly Arthur-style picnic in Russell Square. She took a job in Holborn that year so that she could walk up Southampton Row and have lunch with him in the park between his lectures. Or sometimes in the British Museum, if it was raining. She's slept with a lot of men, or a lot anyway given her conservative origins, but Arthur was the only one she could legitimately call a boyfriend. An echo of his crossover Nigerian/English public school accent catches at her ears, and she wonders what he is doing now. It is sad to have had so many lunches, so many rainy afternoons in the British Museum, and now not even a telephone number. Perhaps she should have married him and made whatever concessions he wanted. But how can you ever really know, when the heart is bewildered, if a decision or a non-decision was the right way to go? Although this thing – this turning of backs on lovers, this severing of ties – is only usual behaviour for her generation. And for her especially, because of feeling easily trapped.

There is still nothing written on her onion-skin paper. The photograph she is looking at now is her seventeen-year-old self in a wintry London. There are two piles on the cotton square in front of her, the perused stack thick, the unperused slender. She is getting to the bottom of the pile. She breathes steadily, sips at the now cold coffee, recognising that she has come to where danger lies. She picks up the London photograph and sets it quickly face-down on the growing heap.

What was the start of things?

In the revealed picture, Lally and Fat Betty are sitting on the stone steps of the veranda of the girls' division, just outside the dining room. Fat Betty's pudgy face is naked and hopeful, Lally's more guarded. It is hard to tell their exact age – they are past puberty but look astonishingly young, their faces still holding the formless dewiness of children. Is it possible that she was ever so young? They must be at least fifteen because they are both wearing burgundy plastic circles on their blazers that signified academic honours only attainable in Standard Eight. Perhaps they are in Standard Eight because they don't seem to have much tin, but then Lally can't remember ever having much tin, and she doesn't imagine Fat Betty did either.

The child Lally's face is elfin and hollow in a way that makes the adult Lally, who is still a thin woman, catch her breath. The child was emaciated. How was it not noticed? But then she recollects that it was noticed – and the noticing took the form of matron's register and the top table. Her stomach flutters delicately. She looks up and away from the picture, catching the waiter's eye. He raises his brow.

'More coffee, please,' she says, aware as she speaks that her voice is not steady and she is trembling a little bit.

There is another figure in the photograph. In the background, a *sisi* is cleaning the dining room windows. Windows day, thinks Lally. The sisi has her back turned to the camera. Lally can't tell which sisi it is – hers or another. The sisi is just a blue overall, a blue *doek*, slippers, a plump bottom, stout, smooth, brown forearms and calves.

They are the forearms and calves of a young woman. Not a girl, but a woman at the height of her physical endurance and strength. Lally peers at the photograph. How old would her sisi have been? She works it out. Even if there had been older children in the family, it is unlikely that the sisi would have been more than thirty-four or thirty-five. All the sisis were from the farms. She would have married and begun child-bearing as an adolescent.

Lally is thirty-five herself. She has thought sometimes about what it would be like to have a baby, a newborn, a toddler. But what would it be like to have a boy of that age, a boy who is almost a grown-up but not a grown-up? And then she thinks, what would it be like to lose him?

'Coffee,' says the waiter, returning. She watches him in silence as he lowers the fresh cup to the table, not spilling, and scoops up her old one.

She picks up the pen and bends over the onion-skin paper and puts the pen down again. How can she say 'the boy was in the shed for one week, and then the security police came and got him'? Because that was only the one thing – the final thing; the big thing. It wasn't the start of things. She feels she must tell it from the start, but the start of things was so many different things.

She thinks: *what was the start?*

She writes: 'I knew Nomda Qhashane better than the other cleaners because she was a kind woman and she noticed me.'

Is. *The thing which I ask I wish for the memory of my child and for my own rest.* She is a kind woman. Lally balls the paper and drops it under the table. On the fresh sheet she writes: 'I was sixteen-and-a-half, and I was a light sleeper.'

A light sleeper. Ridiculous. What a ridiculous thing to say. She reaches into her handbag and pulls out a letter, the second letter, the official one from the Truth Commission with the green, black and gold logo on the left-hand side. She has been carrying it around for six weeks now, and it is a little the worse for wear, with a soft, cloth-like fold to it. But there are the names: Sipho Qhashane, Mrs Nomda Qhashane. And the date, November 18th, and the place, Community Centre, New Brighton Township, Port Elizabeth. Lally must write the words – the memory – in this letter, and in another six weeks the letter will be read out at the Community Centre.

But how? The memory comes from the private space – the most private – secluded behind the scars of concealment, the not-speaking of it. She has never spoken about it to anyone. The attempt to speak to Preston about it was more of a not-speaking, because he remembered some other thing that bore no relation to what she remembered. Now this commission will haul it into the public space. She has seen footage of commission hearings on British television: crowded halls stuffed with packs of journalists, television and radio crews. Members of parliament, translators, the tired small scarlet figure of the archbishop, those who did and those who were done unto. All using the terminology

of which the divisions are unclear to her victims, per-
petrators, beneficiaries. Even if it is only the reading of a
letter, it is her letter, her words, her life, her past. How can
what has been so entrenched in the private space move so
defiantly to the public space?

But Mrs Nomda Qhashane will be giving evidence. And
Mrs Nomda Qhashane was the one who said 'you must
never tell'.

Lally reaches into her handbag again and pulls out another, larger, manila envelope. The envelope is full of press
clippings from the commission. Lally has lied to Pim. She
does not disparage the *Mail & Guardian* and, although
the commission confuses her in many ways, she has been
paying close attention to it. She buys the *Mail & Guardian* every week from a speciality shop that deals in foreign
newspapers, and retains the pages on the commission.

Lally sorts through the contents of the envelope until she
finds the clipping that she is looking for. Because there is
one whom she knows. He has applied for amnesty.

He is not an important amnesty-seeker. He never killed
anyone famous. He merits only a small, grainy picture in a
row of other such pictures. In the black-and-white photograph, the eyes are pale rather than golden, and their glow
is lost. She stares at him in the picture as she could never
dare to stare at him in the flesh. The pose is defiant and – is
it possible? – a little amused. He is an older man now, but
still small and sculpted, and still the *snorretjie*, the small
moustache. Underneath the picture they have reproduced
his name and, as with some of the other pictures, his township nickname, his killing nickname. *Die Luiperd.* Even
reduced to a picture viewed in a foreign land, he seems
vital, controlling, capable of producing fear. She almost
expects the picture-Luiperd to raise his out-of-frame hand
and preen his *snorretjie*.

The *Mail & Guardian* provides a short resume of Die Luiperd's career and his reasons for seeking amnesty. The abduction and murder of Sipho Qhashane is not listed amongst these reasons. But the article reveals that the brigadier saw active service with the police anti-guerrilla unit, *Koevoet*, in South West Africa, where he rose from the rank of lieutenant to colonel. In 1978, he was promoted to brigadier, seconded out of Koevoet and transferred to the Eastern Cape.

Lally rubs her eyes. Despite all the coffee, she feels exhausted. The Eastern Cape. The backwater. The dumping-ground. It has become clear from past amnesty trials and investigations what the Eastern Cape represented to the apartheid government, at the height of its powers. It represented discretion.

They sent them there – the ones like Die Luiperd, the ones who had tasted blood, had seen action in the counter-insurgency units. The ones who were too mad, or too cruel, or whose self-control gave way to blood-instinct at the opportune moment. The ones who might kill a boy who they were only trying to torture – a teenager, too young to have any real information. They sent them there, to those isolated farmlands of the former frontier in the heartland of the country, with its community of complicit whites and cowed blacks, to cool their heels far from the limelight. Because even the most indecent system in the world had some notion of how decency should appear.

'DON'T BATTER BEAGLES! DON'T BATTER BUNNIES! DON'T BATTER BEAGLES! DON'T BATTER BUNNIES!'

Lally's head bucks up from the paper. She stares bewildered at the empty lane outside. Then, around the corner and past her window, come a stream of marchers. The marchers are dressed in loose patterned clothing with dreadlocked hair, or hair concealed under woollen skullcaps knitted in stripes of bright colours. They have on shoes made from rubber and cotton. Some of the women wear close-fitting filmy clothes that accentuate their breasts and hips, with geometric designs at the hem and the end of the sleeves. Silver jewellery glints from their necks, ears, eyebrows and noses. They carry banners depicting tortured dogs and rabbits, with slogans: ENOUGH BLOODSHED FOR VANITY! and IS YOUR BEAUTY WORTH IT? Beneath the banners, the young, angry faces are set and determined – lips pursing on the alliterative chant. They are stopping passers-by to sign their petition – old ladies in sensible coats who shake their heads, not wanting to be involved in whatever this is. Some of the marchers break off from the mainstream and go into the shops to look for more signatories. They don't come into the restaurant, perhaps because of the tinted windows, although the waiter goes outside to sign the petition. They pass a few inches from Lally, but are unaware of her, so that she can watch closely, easily, the rough-spun jerseys, the home-made banners, the red, green, blue, gold, orange and purple strands of colour dyed into their hair. In the wake of the march follows a huddle of older people, in jeans and leather shoes, who evidently agree with the concept of the march, but are unsure about its main body. They carry clipboards, but not banners, and Lally watches them enter into brief, encouraging conversations with the pedestrians about the importance of the petition. The older people glance away from their conversations intermittently, aware that the march is progressing without them – the 'Don't batter beagles and bunnies' war-cry growing fainter – and at last have to apologise and hurry on.

The tight phalanx of the colourful people disappears around the next corner, followed by the more disassembled troupe of older people.

'Activists,' Lally thinks. 'British activists.'

And chuckles, unexpectedly, because the thought of activists for bunnies is quite funny. She tries to stifle the chuckle because it is not really amusing, the cut-up bunnies of the banners probably need the activists. Suddenly, into her mind's eye comes the image of Jeffrey Benzien illustrating his wet-bag technique at the Truth Commission, except instead of demonstrating on a black volunteer, she pictures Benzien's heavy-set form crouched over a bunny.

The chuckle turns into hard, uncontrollable laughter. The waiter, who has come back inside, glowers at her, offended, thinking that she is laughing at the activists. She shakes her head, unable to explain, unable to stop the laughter, and the laughter judders and hiccups and becomes tears. She heaves away from the table, with its display of photographs and clippings and writing materials, and runs to the bathroom.

In the bathroom, she cries for a long time in the toilet stall. Their faces rise up in front of her: the victims, Sipho Qhashane, Mrs Nomda Qhashane; the perpetrator, Die Luiperd; and the beneficiary of the system, herself, her then-self, a skinny, solitary sixteen-year-old girl in a cubicle, the almost-spectator/almost-participant in a backwater murder mystery.

When she is calm again, she emerges from the stall. She stands in front of the mirror. Her dark eyes are sad and swollen, but also, somehow, relieved.

'What are you going to do if you don't run?' she says softly to the mirror-Lally and watches the mirror-woman wince. She touches the reflection of her cheek. 'You can't spend the rest of your life crying in bathrooms.'

Maybe it will be all right if these commission people know the crying. Maybe that is why there is a commission – to cry, to write the letters, to let the words out. God knows, they must all have their own things to cry about too.

She cleans up her face with a damp paper towel and goes back to the table, ignoring the hostile waiter. She draws a breath and reaches for her pen and the pad of onion-skin paper.

She will start, as life itself starts, with a physical fact.

Lally writes: 'There was a shed, next to The Plots'.

Making an Application

The last time she was home was five-and-a-half years ago, because her father had a dragging form of cancer and she needed to help her parents move off the farm and into a small house in the town.

An awkward time; her father depressed, her mother terrified, the endless trips between the dusty provincial town and the farm in the bakkie, weighed down with furniture and bouncing uncontrollably along the rutted roads with their corrugations like the edges of laundry basins. Having lost Arthur. Her mother so mournful. 'Isn't there anyone special? Nobody at work?' Although her mother would not have liked Arthur.

The outgoing white government squabbling and manoeuvring for the last scraps of privilege. Blood and killing in Natal and on the Witwatersrand, burgeoning stories of coteries of killers on whose shadowed lives spotlights began to focus. And then Chris Hani, slaughtered on his doorstep. Lally, in front of the television, felt afflicted by cancers within and without and flew out a week later. On the aeroplane, she felt guilty and weak but relieved. When the drinks trolley arrived, she ordered a Bloody Mary, sinking into a reverie of reflection peculiar to aeroplanes.

On one of the furniture-loading trips, Lally and her mother had passed a column of young girls in grey school uniforms, lolling along the grassy verges of the road. They were from the coloured primary school, the Lettie Hoffman, situated on the neighbouring farm to Lally's. The Lettie Hoffman is a social project of Lally's mother and her friends, who send baskets of old clothes and help to organise sports day and extra supplies of chalk.

Lally, who was driving, glanced at the rear-view mirror whose silver rectangle reflected the children's waving and shrieking. Cars were infrequent on this rural road and each one was a game.

She turned to her mother:

'Why didn't you send me to school with the coloureds? When there was a school so close?'

'I did make an application.' said the elderly woman.

Lally didn't believe her.

'When?' she asked.

'That first term when you came home and you seemed so unhappy, I wrote to the minister and asked for permission to have you at the Lettie Hoffman until you were a little older. I was refused.'

At the farmhouse, the chairs and tables were scattered in a general confusion, with old newspapers and debris everywhere, but Lally's mother cast about in the bottom of a wardrobe and found a cardboard file from which she drew out a yellowed sheet of paper, letterheaded with the national emblem of antelopes and lions. Underneath that was the official stamp of the educational ministry. Lally read:

Dear Madam

With reference to your recent request, we are afraid that we cannot accommodate your child in an educational facility designed for non-whites.

While many children experience some difficulties when first transferring from the home environment to a residential facility, I am sure you will appreciate the greater harm that would result to the wellbeing of the child were a situation allowed to occur such as that suggested by yourself.

With regards
Jacobus van Tonder
Minister of Education
Cape Department

The tomato juice was rich and salty, the Tabasco sauce pungent, the vodka invigorating. Lally stared out of the oval of window at the dark expanses of veld below, with their sporadic punctuation marks of farm lights.

Ruth in the Living Room

When Pim lets himself in through his front door, he hears the rowdy burr of the television. He crosses over to the living room and sees Ruth on the sofa, her head resting on the arm, her feet tucked away underneath her bottom. Mark left a few days ago, which has made the house feel like a sanctuary.

Pim says 'Darling,' and leans to kiss Ruth, but she moves her head at the last moment so it turns into an air-kiss. He eyes her cautiously and looks around for the boys.

'I've put them to bed already. They were tired and grumpy.'

There is an edge to her voice. Pim looks at his watch. It is nine o'clock.

'I do wish,' says Ruth plaintively, 'that you wouldn't always work so late.'

'Oh, Ruth! Who do you think would take care of us if I wasn't motivated to work?'

'But I can't see why you can't keep more reasonable hours. I make supper for you, and you aren't even here to eat it. And besides, it isn't good for you. You'll end up like Richard Fairweather.'

Richard Fairweather is a friend of Pim and Ruth's who developed a stress-related neurosis and had to spend several months recovering at a resort in Spain. Pim looks at Ruth with a mixture of annoyance and contrition, which is achievable because actually he has been working late tonight. He sits beside her on the sofa and tells her a little of his mercantile affairs, which he doesn't do frequently because she isn't usually very interested. But now she does ask him a couple of questions and cradles her head on his shoulder. He slides his hand under her shirt to her breasts.

'Especially when the baby comes,' murmurs Ruth, trying to hold onto her petulance, which is being undermined by an unexpected surge of desire. Pim's hands are swarming over her body, her round bottom, her not-yet-showing stomach.

'No Mark,' says Pim thickly in her ear. 'No boys. Where's Hanka?

'Janka.' He always gets the name of the au pair wrong. 'Out with her boyfriend.' She knots her fingers in his still-thick, grey-blonde hair. 'Don't you want to eat?'

'Later,' says Pim.

Lally in the garden

'This has to stop.' Pim practised various announcements all the way over in the cab. This wasn't the one he settled on, but it is the one that has come out. This morning, an hour ago, he woke up and studied Ruth sleeping next to him on the pillow, and there was an animal of remorse in his throat, clogging his breathing, clawing into his stomach. Then a thunder on the stairs and the boys flying through the door and on to the counterpane, and Pim knew he had made a decision.

'I know,' says Lally. At her feet, the lawn is brittle with night-settled cold, untidily patterned with blown leaves. She releases what is a long breath rather than a sigh and looks up through narrowed eyes at the thinning beech tree. Silly to be outside, really, but when Pim arrived she recognised his purpose and led him through to the garden.

Pim is awaiting a further reaction, stirring his brogues in the leaves, his eyes trained on his flexing hands. The cab is marking time outside. Pim felt he should have this business done with as soon as possible to avoid hedgings and delays that might arise during the course of the day and compromise his decision. When she doesn't speak, he sneaks a look at her. She looks concentrated in another dimension, like someone absorbed in the movie at a cinema. He touches her hand and she moves her cheek against her shoulder, giving him a flat, enquiring look. She doesn't seem happy, but she certainly isn't devastated. Pim feels relieved, but also aggrieved. Surely news of the termination of his services as a lover deserves a more heightened reception? Tears at least.

'Jesus, Lally.' In his head, the softness of Ruth and the hardness of Lally makes a jumble-image, a helter-skelter of impressions, but he knows what a man needs from a woman, or anyway what he needs.

'You're a stone, Lally.' he tells her.

She shrugs.

Lally's mother

If it's lunchtime in England, it's early afternoon in South Africa, and Lally phones deliberately at the time she knows her mother will be napping in order to catch her, but also because Greenbow is at his *charcuterie* and the younger agents are out with clients. She has to use Greenbow's phone because it is the only one with an international line. She keeps an eye on the glass rectangle of the front door as she leans her hand on the broad leather desk that is his work-station. While the phone peals, she pictures her mother flustering awake, registering the intrusion, puttering over the wooden floors in her house slippers. 'Yes?' comes the sleepy voice, a shade annoyed for the interruption. The cracked voice of a widow moving towards seventy with back pains and occasional arthritis, a dead husband, an absent daughter.

'It's me, Mum.'

'Lally!' A glad exclamation. Followed more cautiously by: 'How are you, my dear?'

'I'm fine. I'm coming home.'

'Oh!' A little rush of air as her mother fumbles for the right response. 'Well, that is – well, I am so pleased.' More wakeful now and in command. 'Will you stay for Christmas, do you think?'

'Yes.' The syllables bounce along the international line so she can hear a hollow echo of every word she utters. 'I haven't made any particular plan. But for the summer, at least.'

'I see.' Her mother's voice is both arch and unmasked, trying to discover without appearing to pry. But she sounds encouraged. The summer, in its entirety, is five or six months.

When Lally hangs up, she flicks a paper clip at the area chart on the opposite wall, visualising unenthusiastically the histrionic fuss that Greenbow is sure to make when she informs him of her resignation on his return from lunch.

Pim at work

Throughout the course of the day, Pim experiences a tremendous feeling of release and, concurrently, a resurgence of appreciation for Ruth. Little memories and recollections of Ruth keep surfacing, things he hasn't thought of in years, Their honeymoon in Zanzibar, how shy she was when they first met, how enchanted he was by her soft, silvery voice and the courageous, absurd remarks she came up with to mask her reticence and her attraction.

This genial mood persists into the afternoon, when Pim has arranged to meet a potential client for a sizing-up lunch. Pim's candour infects the client, who as it turns out spent part of his boyhood in Africa, and the conversation somehow slides away from assets and economies and into a romanticised series of abstractions on childhood and Africa and innocence. When they part, both men shake hands, feeling vaguely embarrassed but imbued with that valuable trading commodity – goodwill.

During the afternoon, Pim's thoughts turn to Lally. It is hard to know what to make of her. He sees her as she was this morning, her narrow eyes trained on the beech tree, slim shoulders suggesting that disappointment and failure are too inevitable even to cause regret. Towards the end of the affair, he found her irritating; so self-absorbed, in a universe where people grappled daily with far greater problems than she had ever had. Looking back on it now, he doesn't even really understand why he was with her. Perhaps it was because she was bright. Whatever you said or thought, you could feel it being turned over behind those dark eyes. And she would disagree with him sometimes and put across her own point of view, which was refreshing. Ruth, for the most part, accepts everything he says, and if it is too conceptual, she simply switches off.

But he's in contact with clever women all the time at work and, if he's been tempted to take them to bed, he's never gone through with it. And those are high-flyers. What has Lally ever achieved?

Let's admit it, Pim says to himself, it was a background

thing. But why? After all the distancing, all the releasing, why would he want to? But he did want to, in the face of logic. Pim's hands start to flex, and he shakes his head. Even himself, in making a go of things, had not always found it simple to let go of certain legacies. Although he has come a long way. There is England, Ruth, the boys, the bank, substantiality. Ruth, thank God, is more or less completely ignorant of South Africa. And the boys, with their clear little voices, their mackintoshes, the miniature suits Ruth picks out for them at the children's dress shops in New Kings Road, are British boys. Thinking of his boys, a catch comes into the back of Pim's throat. The boys, and the new baby, if it is a male, will go to prep school, Harrow, Oxford. They will never in their lives wear fatigues, hold a rifle, fight a war. Pim will make sure of it. An English father, in England.

Yes, he has come a long way. And, in thinking of the distance he has travelled, Pim feels contented and serene.

Heathrow

On the tube on the way to Heathrow, Lally berates herself for being late, but when she arrives at the check-in counter the queue is not so sizeable. Before long, all the mandatory questions about firearms and gas canisters and neglected baggage have been asked, and her bags delivered and her seat allocated and there is still an hour to spare before boarding.

She wanders through to the duty-free section and buys a cup of coffee at one of the snack shops and a hamburger from a hamburger chain, which strikes her as tasting particularly dry and unattractive. She thinks cynically that at least the chain doesn't have a franchise in South Africa, although it occurs to her that perhaps it does now. *Five years is a long time. I don't know those kind of details any more.*

She buys her mother a bottle of Opium at the perfumes and tobacco shop and is considering who else to get a Christmas present for when she realises there isn't anyone else who would consider it an obligation.

She has not kept in touch with old school friends; has only the sketchiest idea what became of them. Fat Betty, she heard, had married straight after a secretarial school course and had a baby, which must be an adolescent by now. That musical boy, Welford, who was sometimes called Zulu for a joke, plays for the Cape Town Symphony Orchestra and lectures in wind instruments at the university. And there is Michael, but she would rather not be reminded of Pim for a while.

She gathers together a diverse pile of reading material – *Cosmopolitan, The Spectator*, and a span of dailies of contrasting political leanings. She settles herself on a plush chair in the midst of a row of seats and starts to pick at the collection – an article on the collapse of sheep farming, a tongue-in-cheek self-revelation by a journalist personality, love advice. Winter fashions.

On the farm, the veld will be bleached and parched from the passage of winter, crying out for the summer rains. The fury of the rains; that inspired, decadent sluicing into dust furrows and the next day little mud-pans all over the farm, speckled with animal and bird tracks. If the rains come. Such unpredictable rain – unlike English rain, which is reliable, monotonous, unwanted.

Her thoughts are interrupted by the clamour of young voices and she sees that a crowd of boys is issuing into the waiting area. She recognises them as South African by their accents, and supposes they are on her flight. They must be about sixteen or seventeen years old, a dozen of them, all wearing identical red jerseys bearing the legend:

STANDARD NINE HISTORY TOUR
EASTLEIGH HIGH SCHOOL
OCTOBER '98

Each with a coat of arms underneath consisting of an open book and a wriggling snake. She watches their joking and rambunctious milling as a harassed-looking teacher directs them to the empty row of seats opposite her, thinking that they must have come over for their spring holiday and are now heading back for the fourth term. Mainly white children, although a handful of coloureds or Cape Malays and one black boy. When did the schools integrate? It must have been six, maybe seven years ago.

Most of the boys sitting in front of her have sporty rucksacks hanging off their shoulders, but the black child has a chunky tartan duffel bag. The humour of the bag is obviously already established because, as she watches, a ginger-headed boy whose face is pointillesque with freckles pretends to lift it up and makes a moaning, thwarted noise. The black child pulls the bag away and the ginger child hauls it back, and the black child appears to surrender before administering a final tug, which causes the ginger child to stumble violently over the black child's knees with a winded squawk of surprise.

'Vincent!' spits the beleaguered master. 'Julius! How many times do I have to tell you to *settle down*?'

The boys' faces assume a glazed mask of contrition, innocence and protest. Then the master is elsewhere and they are eyeing each other collusively, lips pressed shut, shoulders trembling.

'British Airways flight zero-five-nine to Johannesburg,'

calls the announcer, 'now boarding at gate thirty-nine.'

'Right, boys,' says the master, flicking the sheath of boarding passes he's confiscated, 'please check you've got all your hand luggage, one at a time through the gate, and no monkey business.' He gives the miscreants a final warning look and the group moves off – more subdued now, perhaps at the thought of returning to school in a day or two.

Lally picks up her own bags and follows in their wake.